THE BONE GARDEN

the Bone Garden

HEATHER KASSNER

TITAN BOOKS

The Bone Garden
Print edition ISBN: 9781789091786
E-book edition ISBN: 9781789091793

Published by Titan Books
A division of Titan Publishing Group Ltd
144 Southwark Street, London SE1 0UP
www.titanbooks.com

First Titan edition: July 2019
10 9 8 7 6 5 4 3 2 1

This is a work of fiction. Names, places and incidents are either
products of the author's imagination or used fictitiously. Any
resemblance to actual persons, living or dead (except for
satirical purposes), is entirely coincidental.

A CIP catalogue record for this title is available from the British Library.

Printed and bound by CPI Group (UK) Ltd, Croydon, CR0 4YY.

What did you think of this book?
We love to hear from our readers. Please email us at:
readerfeedback@titanemail.com, or write to us at the above address.

To receive advance information, news, competitions, and exclusive offers
online, please sign up for the Titan newsletter on our website:
www.titanbooks.com

For my gram, who read me Grimm

I

The Underside of the Graveyard

She descended into the basement, tasked with collecting
the bones. In her hand, a single candle illuminated the
way. It cast a small circle of golden light that pressed the
deepest shadows into the corners.

Not that the dark bothered Irréelle. She could see quite
well in even the blackest part of the night, and besides, she
knew her way around the house by heart, especially this area
so far beneath the floorboards. She carried the candle as
much to guide her as to warm her, if only a little. Her gray
smock dress was too thin for the chill of the cellar.

At the bottom of the staircase, she cupped her hand
to guard the flame. A draft (that seemed to come from
nowhere, but most certainly came from somewhere) blew

cold against her face. It whispered through the white strands of her hair, surrounding her with the scent of earth and rot. She wrinkled her nose. Though she was accustomed to the dank, gloomy basement, it always smelled stronger after the rain.

Irréelle shivered in the enclosed space and reluctantly set the candle down on a stack of wooden crates crammed full of potatoes. She crossed the room, watching her shadow-self stretch ahead. It grew out of proportion to her actual limbs, even taller, even slimmer, her silhouette even more ill composed than her body.

She frowned. The shadow only reminded her of the bony points of her elbows and knees, and worse, the uneven lengths of her arms and the mismatched bones of her legs.

But there was nothing to be done about that except to snub her nose at the shadow.

When she reached the far wall, she placed her hands flat against the bricks, running them over the rough surface until her fingers found the appropriate indentations. Then she pushed down on the grooves as hard as she could. Within the wall, gears began to grind and click. She jumped back and watched as a hidden door groaned open. Beyond it, a long passageway stretched into the darkness. Irréelle could not see to the end.

She retrieved the candle and entered the tunnel. Although the ceiling was higher here, the space crowded tighter. If she held both arms out to the side, she would just be able to touch the walls with the very tips of her fingers.

At eye level along one wall, a shallow metal trough ran the length of the tunnel. She raised the candle, tipping it forward, and touched flame to liquid. The inky black substance at the base of the well ignited. It gave off the scent of tar as it burned, shooting forward in a line of orange flame like a flickering path of lanterns on All Hallows' Eve.

She followed the light. The floor of the passageway sloped downward by the slightest degree the deeper she went underground. Here and there, the thin ends of tree roots poked through from above. She brushed them away as she would a cobweb, very carefully, undisturbed when they swept through her hair or grazed her cheeks.

She hurried along. Back upstairs, and likely none too patiently, Miss Arden Vesper was waiting for her.

Or more precisely, she was waiting for the bones.

Irréelle could not hear her pacing, of course, but she knew that was just what Miss Vesper would be doing. Striding back and forth across the hardwood floor, heels snapping, blue eyes flashing to the clock over the fireplace as it ticked out each second of Irréelle's absence.

At last Irréelle reached the place where the passageway diverged. Six tunnels split off from the first, each of them shrouded in darkness. They branched in different directions, running in parallel lines to the rows arranged so neatly aboveground. Stemming from these passages were other tunnels and niches, outstretched like the thin, jointed legs of a spider holding very still in its web.

She entered the passage on the far left side. It was, perhaps, the oldest of them all, the ground more worn, the walls a little wider.

The maze of tunnels seemed endless, but Irréelle knew where each one led. She wandered through them the way she imagined other children wandered paths in a park. It was not so very different (so long as she pushed away thoughts of the trees and the sky and the fresh summer air). She turned right, then left, then right again, winding deeper into the earth. Here she had only the single candle to light the way and the tug of the bones, which she felt deep inside.

They reached out to her, recognizing her likeness. Their invisible touch was a peculiar feeling, a buzz of static, but so very gentle.

Ahead, candlelight shone upon a crumbling arch, the alcove half caved in and partially blocked by a thick root from what must have been an exceptionally old tree. It was a haunted place. The draft whispered here too, but more insistently, sweeping across her skin and begging for attention. It released a ghostlike sigh, thin and creaky with yearning, as if it searched for some way out and to the surface.

Very purposefully and very quickly, she passed by the opening. Still, she felt the tickle of ghostly fingers and their desire to draw her back. A chill ran down her crooked spine. Never once had she entered this passageway.

It is the wind snaking past, she told herself. Only it felt more like a cold breath against the back of her neck, and she did not want whatever lurked in the gloom to touch her.

Irréelle could not help but glance over her shoulder, watching as the darkness edged across the entrance with each step she took away from it. She felt much better when it was out of sight and she could no longer hear its murmuring.

It was a good thing she did not believe in ghosts, or else she would have certainly thought one lingered there.

She continued walking, mindful of her footsteps even when no one could see her. One stride was just a little bit longer than the other, but she took Miss Vesper's good instruction to *never let her see that awful limp again* and trod more carefully ever after.

The bones hummed to her from every direction. There were so many of them here, and their familiarity warmed her.

She finally came to a stop just outside one of the many shallow recesses equally spaced along the passage. They were not quite twice her length. She lifted the candle to dispel the shadows.

Before her, in the flickering yellow light, was a coffin.

It was one of many caskets from the cemetery above, exhumed from the earth from below. Its lid had long ago been removed, set just beside it on the ground. Candle aloft, Irréelle crossed over to the coffin and peered inside. A skeleton lay peacefully on a bed of tufted blue satin, eye sockets sightless, lower row of teeth missing, finger bones entwined. The folded hands rested upon the rose-printed dress still covering the rib cage.

Irréelle admired the bones, how long they had outlasted the life that once lifted them. She would never tire of visiting. Her own bones shivered beneath her skin as, soundlessly, the skeleton welcomed her.

"Hello," Irréelle said, her voice quiet, ever respectful of the dead. "If you are accommodating, would you permit me to gather your bones?" She tilted her head, ear toward the coffin, and listened.

The skeleton said nothing. And although Irréelle had yet to receive a response to this question on any of her visits to the underside of the graveyard, she always politely asked for permission. She waited a moment longer, giving the skeleton time to consider the request.

When still it remained silent, she bowed her head and placed one hand over its bony fingers. They tingled with a warmth that had surprised her the first time but she understood quite well now. Acceptance. "Thank you. I promise to take only what I need."

Then she put down the candle and dug her tools out of her pockets. She set her collection of small glass vials along the edge of the coffin, except for one. She uncorked this vial and snapped it into place in the long needlelike instrument in her hand, which she called the bone borrower (and which Miss Vesper called the extractor).

She knelt in the dirt beside the coffin. Being a rather small girl, there was just enough space for her to fit.

Leaning forward, she positioned the sharp tip of the bone borrower and pierced the skeleton's skull. Although Irréelle knew it could not feel a thing, she was gentle and considerate of not leaving a mark. She sang softly to cover the faint whirring of the machine as it threaded beneath the surface, turning bone to dust. Soon, the vial filled with a fine white powder. She removed the vial from the bone borrower, capped it securely, and slipped it into her pocket.

She selected another vial and repeated the process on the skeleton's brittle collarbone. Moving from head to toe, in just the order Miss Vesper had taught her, she gathered bits of bone as unobtrusively as she could. It took quite some time, as she worked with such care. When she was through, she stood, brushing the dirt from her knees. In her pockets, the vials clinked against one another, an assortment of dust from each classification of bone.

"Goodbye," she said to the skeleton. "Thank you again."

She walked back the way she had come, a little slower now as the path inclined. When she reached the main passageway, the fire she had lit still burned. The long line of orange flame led her back to the cellar. Once there, she pressed a small lever on the wall, which lowered a cover across the entire well and extinguished the fire.

Ducking through the doorway, she tapped the bricks behind her, pulling her fingers quickly away before the heavy door swinging shut could smash them. It aligned seamlessly with the wall again, sealing off the tunnels, as if they did not even exist.

The rest of the world knew nothing of them, just as it

knew nothing of Irréelle. She took up such a small slip of space that she wondered if she left any imprint at all. Or if she was as unreal as the ghosts she did not believe in.

With a rather crooked gait, she ran ahead of her thoughts. They always got her into trouble, slowing her down when she should have been hurrying.

Up she went, climbing the steep, twisty staircase to the main floor of the house. Faster now, as if she could make up for her delay. From above, the door creaked open, and a sliver of light snaked down like lightning. With it came a gust of wind that blew out her candle's trembling flame.

Outlined on the landing, a shadow spoke.

2

Miss Vesper

Halfway up the staircase, Irréelle froze. She rested her hand on the cold brick wall to steady herself.

"Bring me the bones," the shadow said, and then slipped away. Heels clicked on the floorboards.

She let out a breath. Of course, it was only Miss Vesper come to hurry her along. Again and always, Irréelle had been too slow. She emerged from the cellar, squinting at the brightness of the day streaming through the windows, and stepped into the hallway at the back of the house. Having been so long underground, she stared at the clouds for a moment as they drifted across the blue sky.

But she had no more time for cloud gazing. She glanced down at her dress, which was covered with a fine layer of dust and dirt. She stamped her boots and patted her skirt, glad the fabric was gray and hid the grime (for the most part), and relieved the skirt fell just long enough to cover her dirtied knees.

Before following after the echo of Miss Vesper's footsteps, she withdrew the bone borrower from her pocket. She lifted the corner of her dress and wiped the instrument clean of bone dust, and then put it away, careful not to stab herself in the leg.

As she went down the hall, she ran a hand over her white hair to smooth it behind her shoulders. Although it was perfectly straight, it tended to fall out of place and hang forward across her face.

Miss Vesper waited for her in the study. She stood beside the fireplace, her palms outstretched to warm herself before the blazing hearth. Even though it was summer, the fireplace burned, as it always did. The room smelled of wood and smoke, and through the tall windows came a breeze that stirred the white curtains and carried the scent of lilac. Irréelle hoped it would mask the damp, earthy smell that clung to her clothes.

Slowly, Miss Vesper turned. Her midnight-blue eyes seemed to look through Irréelle, who always felt small and insubstantial next to Miss Vesper.

The clock ticked on the mantel.

"At long last, you return," Miss Vesper said. She lifted a rectangular case onto her desk, snapped up the brass clip that held it shut, and let it fall open. "Set them here."

Irréelle came closer. The warmth from the fireplace sank into her skin. She pulled the vials from her pockets one by one and set them into their snug compartments beside all of the others she had gathered previously. The case's velvet lining was soft beneath her fingertips.

"Very good. Now let me see the extractor." Miss Vesper held out her hand. She had long, thin fingers and pretty, manicured nails painted coral pink. Her diamond ring flashed.

Irréelle passed her the sharp instrument, which contrasted with the woman's dainty appearance despite the fact that Miss Vesper knew exactly how to use the tool and clasped it firmly and confidently. It was only that she looked so proper, so sweet. She wore a slim black dress with sleeves to her wrists, the lace hem to her knees, and black, round-toed heels with a curlicue design stitched into the leather. Her honey-brown hair fell in waves to her shoulders, and her pert nose lent her face a youthful countenance, though she had to be more than twice as old as Irréelle's eleven years.

(Not that she knew her own age exactly, as Miss Vesper

had never told her more than *she was not made by time, but looked like an unpleasant child of just less than a dozen years.*)

Miss Vesper raised the bone borrower to the light. The silver tip shone. She pursed her lips, lowered the instrument, and swiped it casually across her skirt. Irréelle sucked in a breath. Miss Vesper smiled, teeth sharp and white. The faintest trace of bone dust stood out against her black dress.

"I'm sorry," Irréelle said in a rush, standing as straight as she could, trying to mirror Miss Vesper's exacting posture.

"I expect you are." Miss Vesper brushed the tiny particles from her dress. Then she opened the top drawer of her desk and pulled out a handkerchief. She polished the instrument until there was not a single trace of bone dust left, and then placed it in the case beside the vials. "You will have to be more careful."

"I will. I promise."

Miss Vesper did not acknowledge her response; instead she closed the case and refolded the handkerchief so that the embroidered initials were displayed. *N.M.H.* Irréelle did not know what they stood for, only that the initials could be found everywhere around the house. Engraved on the edges of the bone china in the glass-front cabinets. Stitched onto the ivory hand towels. Printed on the stationery that sat atop Miss Vesper's desk. And, though it was faded and hard to make out, painted on the mailbox to the left of the front door.

"You were gone such a very long time today. Far too long."

"I did not mean to keep you waiting."

"I could not bear to be in those claustrophobic tunnels." Miss Vesper shuddered, but just as quickly she went very still, as if she did not want Irréelle to notice the tiny crack in her composure. "However, I imagine you must have enjoyed yourself, dallying as you did."

Although it was not a question, Irréelle knew it was best to apologize once again. "I'm sorry I was not faster."

"It's like picking flowers, isn't it, collecting such pretty things from the bone garden?" Miss Vesper's fingertips grazed the daffodils sitting in the vase on her desk. The yellow petals wilted by the smallest degree at her touch. She drew her hand back without seeming to notice.

Irréelle could not remember a time she had ever picked flowers. She so rarely left the house at all, and when she did she only ventured as far as the backyard. Even then, she kept beneath the oak tree's bowed branches, careful not to let the neighbors see her.

Miss Vesper rounded the desk and grasped Irréelle's hands in her own. She was unused to Miss Vesper coming so close, even more to being touched. The kindness of the gesture startled her. It could be nice, she decided, it could be comforting. If only Miss Vesper's fingers were not so icy. Knots tightened in Irréelle's stomach.

"I simply wish you worked faster." Miss Vesper sighed. "But I suppose the fault is my own." Her grip tightened, the tips of her nails digging into Irréelle's palms. She pulled Irréelle's arms out between them and held them straight. Both arms were scrawny, the right not quite as long as the left. "How mismatched you are." She looked into Irréelle's eyes. "How muddled."

Irréelle's eyes were green and brown and gold, and the left one had a dash of blue. She blinked several times, wanting only to close her eyes so Miss Vesper would not have to see them and be so offended by their odd color.

Miss Vesper dropped Irréelle's arms and turned away from her. "Be calm. As I said, the fault is mine." She shook her head. "Or the boy's, wouldn't you say?"

Irréelle clasped her hands behind her back. Whether she agreed or not, she knew how best to reply. "The boy's, I would say."

"Have you seen him, then?"

"I have seen no one." She did not mention the children she sometimes spied through the fence, chasing a dog or throwing a ball back and forth. She might not have known who Miss Vesper was referring to, but it was not those pigtailed girls.

Miss Vesper took a seat in one of the two overstuffed armchairs flanking the fireplace. She did not curl her legs beneath her and sink into the cushions as Irréelle had always longed to do. Instead, she sat like she would at her desk, with her back straight and her legs crossed.

Without an invitation to take the other chair, Irréelle stayed where she was.

"I suppose that is neither here nor there. And now you are here and he is there."

Irréelle nodded. A few strands of hair fell forward into her face and she left them there, grateful for something to hide behind.

"It's a shame you are so strange, and weak too. I had another task in mind for you."

It always came back to this, the task she could not perform. "I am not so weak." Outwardly she may have looked unfinished, as if there were not enough colors to fill in all her lines, but the inside of her felt bright and sharp. Even if Miss Vesper could not see it.

Miss Vesper looked her up and down. "But as I said, you are so strange."

Irréelle knew that better than anyone. She pressed her knees together, though they did not align, but nothing could prevent her trembling. Miss Vesper's voice cut deeper.

"With you, I had quite enough imagination, but not enough bone dust." Miss Vesper swiped at invisible specks on her dress. Then she closed her eyes and tilted her head. The light fell across her face, emphasizing the lovely angle of her cheekbones. "I imagined a smart girl, small and quick, with black hair, sparkling eyes, delicate features, and strong, strong bones." Her eyes snapped open and focused on Irréelle. "You *are* small."

The words stung, no matter that they were true. Irréelle's cheeks burned. Miss Vesper might have slapped her and it would not have hurt so much. "Perhaps I can be mended and made right."

"No, no. Certainly not. I could not spare the time nor the bone dust. It is far too precious, and you are too odd to be helped."

"Perhaps I am useful still." Irréelle glanced down at herself. "As I am."

"As you are? Absolutely not." Miss Vesper ran a finger along her eyebrow, though it was already arched and smooth. "Why, if anyone were to catch sight of you, they would not even know what to make of your freakish form.

No matter the importance of this task, I could never risk sending you out into the world. What would people think of me if they knew I created a creature such as yourself? You haven't thought of the trouble you might bring to my door. You are a selfish thing."

Irréelle did not like to dwell on the unusual manner in which she was made, but of course Miss Vesper was right. If anyone were to see Irréelle (and they did not immediately faint from fright), they would be suspicious of her nature and wonder from where she came. The last thing Irréelle wanted to do was cause Miss Vesper any harm. "I only wanted to help."

"That may be, but what you want is of little concern to me. Off you go, then."

Irréelle was breathing very fast, doing her best to keep the tears from spilling past her pale eyelashes. She turned to leave, wanting to run from the room so Miss Vesper would not see her cry, but she walked toward the door as if nothing were wrong. One foot already in the hallway, Irréelle paused when Miss Vesper spoke again.

"Remember, my dear, you do not really and truly exist. You are a figment of my imagination, tethered here by the finest thread."

3

The Measure of a Girl

Alone beneath the oak tree, she watched tears splash into her lap. She told herself to stop, but the tears refused to obey and continued to stream down her cheeks and through her fingers held up to her face.

For all the cruel things Miss Vesper had ever said to her (that she no doubt deserved), this last reminder was the one that hurt most deeply: that Irréelle might not exist outside of Miss Vesper's own mind and could be thought away, if only she closed her blue eyes and wished it. *Much like smashing a bug underfoot*, she had explained to her once, stomping her heel to the floor for effect.

Thinking of it again, Irréelle winced. Her stomach squirmed like a poor smooshed bug wiped from the bottom of Miss Vesper's shoe. In a different but equally horrible manner, Miss Vesper might wipe Irréelle from her mind and turn her back to dust.

Irréelle sniffed and dried her eyes. Tears would only anger Miss Vesper, and all Irréelle wanted was to please her.

She lowered her hands and held them out in front of her. They were perfectly proportionate, one to the other, and because of this Irréelle often thought they looked out of place compared with the rest of her body and all its irregular lines. She turned her hands this way and that. They looked real enough to her. When she wanted them to move, they moved, turning a page in a book when she finished a chapter, handling the bone borrower in its delicate work, pulling blades of grass from the lawn.

Without quite intending to, Irréelle found herself clenching fistfuls of grass. She opened her hands and blew across her palms. The blades scattered, sprinkling to the ground.

From the yard behind her house came a sudden peal of laughter. Her gaze darted to the wooden fence separating the houses. She climbed to her feet and walked over to the bushes surrounding a white-bloomed hawthorn. Behind them, she found the section of the fence where one of the wooden planks had split, and through it she could see into the other yard. Pushing to her tiptoes, she shut one eye, and with the other, she peered through the crack and caught the pigtailed girls at play, red-faced with laughter.

Her bones twinged the way someone else's heart might ache.

They were not aware of her in the least.

They did not even know she existed.

If they peered over the fence, Irréelle wondered if they would see right through her, or if they would shriek at the oddness of her body and run screaming to their parents. She was not sure which was worse. All the same, she watched them.

One girl lay flat on her back in the overgrown grass, arms and legs splayed. She seemed to be doing nothing more than staring at the sky. The other girl spun in circles, arms out to her sides, pigtails sticking straight out from her head. Her skirt billowed around her. The faster she turned, the more off balance she became, though she fought to remain upright as long as she could, until she stumbled and her legs collapsed beneath her. She fell, dizzy and laughing, to the ground, landing in a heap beside the girl who must have been her sister (they looked quite alike). They rested so near that their fingers brushed against each other.

Irréelle pressed her face closer to the fence despite the rough, splintery wood grating against her cheek. She thought that, just maybe, their pinkies linked together, though it was hard to say for sure given the distance.

"I could do this all day long," said the first girl.

"I'm seeing double," said the second girl. She slapped a hand to her forehead as if to hold her vision still.

"Do you see two of me, then?" the one said to the other, leaning over her sister and making a rather silly face with her tongue sticking out of her mouth.

"Yes, unfortunately," the other said to the one.

The first girl ignored this comment. "Again!" she said, jumping to her feet. Loose strands of hair escaped from both pigtails.

Soon they were twirling in circles again, one clockwise, the other counterclockwise. Somehow, they managed not to crash into each other. They seemed to be enjoying themselves immensely, yet Irréelle's stomach flipped just thinking of revolving so quickly, and worse, losing her footing. She did all she could to deflect notice, and the last thing she would want to do was spin and lurch in such a way as to call more attention to her body's imbalance.

Except the girls made it look so *fun*, so carefree, like their appearance did not matter at all. They did not give it a second thought, not the disarray of their hair, not the grass stains on their skirts, not the flailing of their limbs. Maybe they would not even think her so odd. Sometimes she tried to imagine what it would be like to say hello to them, but she knew she would never gather the courage.

If only she had someone to call a friend, just as the sisters had each other. She would not care what they looked like or if they were made of dust and bone. All that would matter was that they were kind.

Irréelle did not wait to watch the sisters fall. She drew back from the fence and disentangled herself from the lilac bush, pushing the hawthorn's low-hanging branches out of her way. At her back the girls laughed again, until they were breathless.

* * *

Much, much later that night, after she had scrubbed herself clean and eaten dinner alone in her room, and when she was almost certain Miss Vesper would not need her for anything else that evening, Irréelle closed her bedroom door, knelt on the floor in front of her bed, and pulled out an old, worn box. She lifted the lid and drew out a feather.

It was glossy and black, from either a crow or a raven. Whichever, it must have been a large bird, because the feather was longer than any other she had found before. She ran the silky vane through her fingers. Each of the barbs sprang back into place.

She carried the feather to the fireplace. Embers glowed orange in the hearth and filled the tiny room with warmth. She poked the quill into the coals until the tip darkened with ash.

Hidden on the back of the door, little dashes marked the white paint. She stood in front of the markings, her back pressed flat against the wood, her posture as straight as it could be, her longer leg bent just so. Feather in hand, she brought it overhead and ever so carefully touched quill to door, drawing a line of ash to mark her height.

Stepping back to compare the lines, she realized she had grown by a pinch (give or take a smidgen), which might have been an adequate way to measure salt, nutmeg, or bone dust, but it was not a very accurate way to measure a girl. Without a ruler, she had come to accept that it would have to do.

She had not grown by much. Yet it was enough to satisfy Irréelle. She liked to think she had this secret. That she could change (even in such a small way as this) without Miss Vesper imagining it done.

Still using the feather, she measured the length of her

bones. It tickled the insides of her wrists and the backs of her knees, but she did not laugh or smile. Concentrating on the task, she measured the bones in her legs and the bones in her arms, but no matter how many times she did so, it only confirmed what she could already see with her own muddled eyes. Her limbs did not align.

They might grow longer, but they did not grow evenly. For some foolish reason, she always expected different results and therefore was always disappointed. Irréelle would never look right. Not completely. If she did not want Miss Vesper to wish her away, she would need to be very good and please Miss Vesper with every task.

Maybe, if Irréelle did everything just as she should, Miss Vesper might spare some bone dust after all. She could set Irréelle's bones right. She could imagine her normal.

She could imagine her *real*.

4

For Luster and Longevity

Miss Vesper always slept late. Or rather, Irréelle always woke early, quick to shed the cloak of sleep and the gnawing fear that if she spent too long in the darkness, she might never find her way out of it. It would be so easy to drift away, falling not into dreams but into nonexistence.

She rose before the first hint of morning light, before the chirping of the sparrows and robins replaced the chirping of the crickets and other night creatures. It was a time when those with any sense stayed comfortable in their beds, or for Irréelle (who was a sensible girl), it was a stolen time all her own.

At this hour, drifting soundless down the staircase, the house was quiet and still. She trespassed through the silence, wondering if she ought to wait for the dawn to properly announce the start of the day before intruding upon it. Until it was rightly morning, she felt as if she were passing through a place that looked like, sounded like, and smelled like yesterday. The air was stale.

She slipped into the study. In the hearth, the embers had burned down sometime in the night. She cleaned away the soot and then rebuilt the fire so it would be blazing just in time for Miss Vesper's morning cup of tea.

In the firelight she could not help but notice the sad state of the daffodils, sapped of color and drooping in the center of the desk. They were most decidedly dead.

When she lifted the vase, withered petals fell to the floor in a way that reminded her of autumn leaves tumbling to the ground. She scooped them up and went into the kitchen, thinking of the fact that she had never picked flowers before, which Miss Vesper had referred to so fondly, and decided to replace them.

The back door creaked as she opened it. Stepping outside, she whispered good morning to the bones, trusting the wind would carry her message. Even here, blocks from the cemetery, she felt the gentle pull of them. It seemed as if they were so much closer, their trembling warmth soothing her loneliness.

She followed the path that led around the side of the house, passing the hawthorn and lilacs. A small rose garden grew to the left. To the right, flower beds ran along the fence, daffodils and tulips, lilies and chrysanthemums. With blooms tilted upward, they waited for the first rays of sunshine.

Irréelle bent at the waist and snapped the stem of a tulip between her fingers. Dew clung to the red petals. She chose five more just like it, the brightest she could find, and then three yellow ones as well. In the crook of her arm, she carried them back inside and into the study, filling a vase with fresh water on the way.

She took extra care arranging the flowers, spending many minutes adjusting them this way and that, the yellows placed between the reds, aware of their best angles. Just as she stepped back to admire her work, Miss Vesper entered the room. Irréelle spun around at the sound of clicking heels.

"There you are," Miss Vesper said by way of greeting, as if she had spent all morning trying to find her. In her hand, she held a bone china saucer and cup of tea.

"Good morning," Irréelle replied.

Ever observant, Miss Vesper craned her neck, graceful in even this small movement, and glanced at the new flower arrangement. "Lovely," she said. "If only I did not detest the scent of tulips."

Irréelle edged backward, knocking into the desk. She sniffed the air. "I did not think tulips had any scent at all."

"Precisely. You did not think."

"I will replace them with roses, if you prefer. Or daffodils again." She reached for the vase, but Miss Vesper shook her head.

"That will not be necessary. Leave them." Although the tulips may have been without fragrance, the tea she sipped smelled of mint. "Sometimes, it is enough that you try so very hard to please me." She smiled, and a dimple appeared in one of her cheeks.

Irréelle warmed at the words and felt her face flush. Yet as soon as she received this attention, she felt the need to deflect it. She lifted a small ceramic bowl from the desk and held it up in front of her. "For your tea?"

Miss Vesper took a pinch of the white powder Irréelle offered, which guests, if she had ever had any, might have mistaken for sugar or maybe salt, but was in fact bone dust. It was a very special blend, not for dark imaginings and creations but for Miss Vesper's longevity. She sprinkled it into her tea, dipped her pinkie in the liquid, and stirred it once, then twice, until it had dissolved. Then she tasted it.

Her hair, which had fallen rather limp and dull overnight, brightened and curled, bobbing on her shoulders. And her eyes, glassy from the sleeping serum she drank on restless nights, sharpened.

"Perhaps a dash more," she said, and poured the remaining contents of the little dish into her tea. "However, now I've used the last of this variety, and you will have to gather more." She looked at Irréelle over the rim of the cup as she took another sip. Her ashen cheeks pinked with health.

Irréelle scolded herself silently. She should have collected it yesterday with all the rest. If only she had deeper pockets to fit all the vials. "I will gather more." Irréelle turned to go, but Miss Vesper's voice held her there.

"And do be mindful of wiping your boots when you return. Just look at the dirt you tracked in from outside."

Irréelle looked down at the floor but could see nothing on the hardwood except the small beige-and-blue rug under the desk. But if Miss Vesper saw dirt, then it must be there, for she had a very keen eye.

Miss Vesper set down her cup and saucer. She lifted her hand, narrowed her eyes, and at her command a fine swirl of dirt and dust rose from the soles of Irréelle's boots and also the floor, in exactly the places she had stepped. "Hold out your hand."

The small cloud of dirt swept up from the floor and sprinkled down into Irréelle's palm. Although she had witnessed it many times before, Irréelle always marveled over this strange and spectacular feat, and Miss Vesper's oneness with the earth. No matter how hard she concentrated, Irréelle could not lift a single speck of dust. If only she had an ounce of Miss Vesper's magic, Irréelle might be able to align her crooked body.

"Staring is quite rude," Miss Vesper said.

Irréelle lowered her eyes and closed the dirt in her fist. Mumbling an apology, she turned to go.

"Bring my teacup to the kitchen. I am through with it."

"Yes, Miss Vesper." And thus dismissed, Irréelle fetched the cup with her other hand and slipped out of the room.

As she walked down the hall, the last of the tea sloshed inside the cup. Peppermint scented the air, and Irréelle could almost taste it on her tongue. She bit her lip. Perhaps if she drank it, she too could command the dirt or turn her cheeks rosy.

Oh, she should not have thought it, but as soon as the idea settled in her mind, she could not shake it. Irréelle glanced over her shoulder and scurried into the kitchen. Before Miss Vesper could chance upon her, Irréelle placed the cup to her lips, tipped back her head, and poured the contents down her throat.

Although Miss Vesper did not so much as flinch when she drank it, Irréelle gagged on the chalky grains of bone dust. She had never tasted anything so horrible. Even the mint could not mask the bitterness, but she forced herself to swallow it.

And then she waited and waited for something to happen.

Besides the grittiness on her tongue, she felt no different. Her arms and legs did not correct themselves. Her long strands of hair did not flood with color. And when she opened her fist and focused on the dirt and dust, she still could not move the tiniest piece of it.

Instead of feeling discouraged, Irréelle only felt more determined. *This* blend of bone dust was specially made for Miss Vesper. Somehow, Irréelle would have to convince Miss Vesper to create one just for her.

* * *

Irréelle spent the rest of the day in the underside of the graveyard. This task was more delicate than most, as Miss Vesper was quite particular about the type of dust she took with tea. Irréelle knew the measurements exactly but referred to the list she had written out previously to ensure she made no errors.

MISS VESPER'S BONE DUST BLEND
for luster and longevity

- Jawbone—one thimbleful

- Hipbone (extract borrow from two skeletons)—one vial each, full to the brim

- Rib cage—half a dash

- Ring-finger bone (from the left hand only, for extra sweetness)—a single twist

- Thighbone—one vial

- Cinnamon—one-fourth teaspoon

When she finally crept out of the basement that afternoon, pockets clinking with vials, she cleaned the bone borrower most thoroughly and then went to deliver the bones. Footsteps came from three flights up. Miss Vesper was at work in the attic.

A spiral staircase, made of wrought iron, led up to the

highest room in the house. Irréelle had always thought it beautiful, all of the detailed leaf-work like the lace on her best dress, until Miss Vesper told her the tale of a clumsy girl who did not watch her step and tumbled the entire way down, snapping her neck in her carelessness.

At hearing this horrible story, which Miss Vesper relayed matter-of-factly and without showing a hint of emotion or an ounce of sympathy, Irréelle went cold. Sure enough, she spent many a day beneath the graveyard, but that was somehow different from this long-ago tragedy that had occurred just down the hall from where she slept.

She hopped over the floorboards so as not to step upon the place she imagined the poor girl had fallen. Once she reached the top of the staircase, she knocked on the closed wooden door. Just once. Just a tap.

Moments later, the door swung open. Miss Vesper was already walking away from it, back toward the center of the room and the long wooden table that took up so much space. Across its top rested a small notebook (one Miss Vesper always kept with her), a pencil, and dozens of jars and bowls of varying sizes, holding all manner of liquid and powder. Long rows of shelves lined the attic walls, and on them sat racks of vials and old journals written in a different hand than Miss Vesper's.

Soft light filtered through the skylight. It reflected off the many glass jars.

"Put everything away," Miss Vesper directed. "I will make it later." She selected several vials and tipped them over a large bowl all at once. The contents braided around each other as they fell. "Did you see him this time? The boy?" The question seemed an afterthought, but it was one she had been asking more and more frequently.

"I saw no one," Irréelle said, just as she had the day before (and the day before that as well), with no more understanding of who this boy might be, unless one of the skeletons finally decided to address her or a ghost materialized before her.

When Miss Vesper did not respond, Irréelle went to the shelf beside the door. She set each of the vials she had gathered on one of the racks. As she went to place the last one, her hand froze midair.

The vial was empty. Of all the things to forget, the one ingredient she simply needed to find in the cupboard and measure out with a little spoon.

Before she turned toward Miss Vesper, she smoothed her hair and straightened her skirt. "I seem to have forgotten the cinnamon," she said, not wanting to interrupt Miss Vesper in the middle of her work, but speaking up before she lost her nerve.

Miss Vesper lifted her head, finger to the page to hold her place. "The cinnamon? Well, you are in luck. I needed it for something else and brought it upstairs already." Miss Vesper pointed to one of the stubby jars in front of her.

Irréelle leapt forward. In her haste, her longer leg did not wait for the shorter one, and she staggered about in just the manner Miss Vesper despised. Worse yet, when she saw Miss Vesper's lips press into a thin line, she faltered. The empty vial slipped through her fingertips and shattered into a thousand fragments across the hardwood floor.

5

Breathe

It sparkled like sugar. Irréelle stood perfectly still amid the broken glass. Sweat beaded on her forehead.

Miss Vesper let out an inaudible sigh, her chest rising and then falling its only evidence. She set a black ribbon between the pages of her notebook and closed it. She touched two fingers to the corner of her mouth, as if to stay the words sitting on the tip of her tongue, and then tucked her honey-brown hair behind one ear. Each movement was slow and deliberate. Miss Vesper was nothing if not poised.

"What a terrible mess," she said. "One I cannot imagine away as I could imagine you away."

Irréelle found her mouth too dry to speak. Her legs,

which had been in such a rush to carry her forward, now betrayed her again, only in quite the opposite manner. They would not move a muscle, not even to retreat. She did not want Miss Vesper to imagine her away, but she desperately wanted to disappear.

"Now I see why you are always so dreadfully slow," Miss Vesper said, pouring cinnamon into a vial. "It is all you can do to stay on your own two feet."

Miss Vesper came around the table, heels crunching over the glass, grinding it into smaller and smaller pieces. She put the vial away beside the others and looked over each one Irréelle had so recently filled, tapping the corks to settle the bone dust, as if to catch some small error in measurement.

Although she had been very careful, Irréelle shrank into herself, rounding her shoulders though she usually worked so hard to straighten them. What if she had mixed up the ingredients and instead of gathering one thimbleful of jawbone and half a dash of rib cage, she had instead collected it the other way around? That combination would have been absurd.

However, all must have been in order, as Miss Vesper walked back to the table and opened her notebook. On a blank page, she jotted down a brief notation and then glanced up. "Must I instruct you on how to clean up?"

Miss Vesper did not need to ask her twice. Irréelle shook herself out of the stupor. "I'm sorry. I need no instruction." Her voice came out as a squeak.

She did not know where to place her feet, but stepped as cautiously as she could around the glass and slipped out the door. It took all her willpower to go slowly down the spiral staircase. Now that she was moving, she wanted to run.

From the closet in the hall she grabbed a broom and a dustbin. In the bathroom, she wet an old hand towel. (She knew better than to use one initialed with *N.M.H.*) She lugged everything up to the attic.

Miss Vesper did not give the slightest impression that she noticed Irréelle's return and continued with whatever it was she was doing, which involved mashing a chalky gray substance with a mortar and pestle. It smelled like black licorice.

Irréelle began to sweep up the glass. It had scattered to the far corners of the room and had broken into such fine pieces that she had to go over the entire floor three times with the broom. Even then, she could not be sure she had gotten it all, so she went to her knees and wiped the floor by hand, plank by plank, reaching beneath the cabinets and cleaning under the table, her hand dodging here and there to avoid having her fingers caught under Miss Vesper's toes whenever she took a step.

From the corner of her eye, she watched Miss Vesper. She was no longer stirring or measuring. Instead, she had plopped a ball of gray clay (or something that looked like clay) onto the table and was rolling it out on a layer of bone dust, much as she would roll out cookie dough on a sprinkling of flour. When it was even and flat, she picked up a scalpel and sliced into it.

Without meaning to, Irréelle stopped sweeping. She leaned against the broom, amazed at each intricate cut of Miss Vesper's blade. Whatever she was making, the pieces were small. As she finished shaping them, she placed them on a silver tray, a deliberate arrangement that began to look more and more familiar as each piece was added.

All at once, Irréelle realized what she was looking at. The reconstructed bones of a hand. All twenty-seven of them.

Miss Vesper tipped one of the glass jars and shook out a thin line of cinnamon along the length of each bone-dust finger. Next, she took in her hand something that looked very much like a paintbrush. With it, she dabbed the chalky mixture she had made earlier, and then she touched brush to bone and coated each finger with the thick paste.

"You seem very interested in what I'm doing here. You may as well stop sweeping," Miss Vesper said.

Irréelle looked down at her boots. She had not meant to be so obvious in her curiosity.

"I created you in just this manner, although I will be sure to take more care this time, as I did all the times before you. Now that I have a sufficient amount of bone dust."

Irréelle flinched.

"You must know you are not the first. Had you no idea?" Miss Vesper's blue eyes widened. She added another coat of paste to the bones.

Irréelle had some idea but did not want to voice it and make it true, so all she said was, "I'm not sure I understand."

Miss Vesper laughed. A quiet laugh, covered with the back of her hand. "Who do you think helped create the tunnels? I could not call all that dirt myself."

She had not thought of it. It seemed an underworld that had always existed.

"Who do you think gathered the bone dust before you?"

Irréelle shook her head. In her trembling hand the broom juddered. She gripped it more firmly to keep it still.

"Who do you think gathered the bone dust that *created* you?"

"Someone else, I suppose." It was not a specific

answer, but Irréelle felt the need to say something. However, as soon as the words left her mouth, another thought came to mind. "You asked if I'd seen him. A boy."

"Yes."

Irréelle did not know what had happened to him but suspected it was nothing good if Miss Vesper had been forced to design someone as mismatched as her. She wanted to hear no more lest she end up like him.

Miss Vesper set down the brush only to pick up a pair of scissors with exceptionally long blades. "Come over here."

Dragging the broom behind her, Irréelle did as she was told. She faced Miss Vesper across the table. Without a word, Miss Vesper reached forward. She snipped off a lock of Irréelle's long white hair, which had been very straight across the bottom and was now as uneven as all the rest of her. Her hand went automatically to the ragged ends.

Miss Vesper laid Irréelle's just-cut hair across the repurposed bones. At first nothing happened, but then the strands began to lengthen. They wove and twined together, moving faster and faster, as if invisible hands stitched thread, until the hair completely covered the bones with what looked to be skin.

"As I said, you are not the first, nor will you be the last." Miss Vesper offered these words like a warning.

The threat jabbed Irréelle in the chest and she took a step back. She did not want to be replaced like the unnamed boy and become an unnamed girl.

Miss Vesper leaned closer to the table, her mouth only inches from the hand. She looked thoughtful, as if she were digging up her darkest imaginings. "Breathe," she whispered.

The index finger twitched.

6

The Dust-and-Bone Hand

Irréelle gasped. The Hand looked so lifelike, so much like her own, only it was not attached to any other body parts, of course. Yet still it moved. What was once dust was now bone, what was once cinnamon was now blood, what was once hair (*her* hair) was now skin. It was translucent at first, and then deepened in color like a loaf of bread browning in the oven. The Hand was perfectly formed.

"Hmm." Miss Vesper watched the Hand intently.

It was an appraising look, as if she were only waiting to be disappointed. Irréelle knew that look all too well but was not used to seeing it directed at anyone, or anything, other than her.

The finger twitched again, an awkward movement,

like its joints were stiff and rusty with disuse. It seemed disoriented, as could be expected when it had no eyes to see with. (Although somehow it heard Miss Vesper's command without any ears, which made little sense to Irréelle but she accepted anyway, because really, if she thought too hard about the many peculiar things in the world, she would have no time for anything else.)

The other fingers began to jerk, each in turn. Knuckles cracked, skin stretched over bone. Then the Hand gained more coordination and the spasms eased. The index finger settled beside the others on the table. It touched the wooden surface, sliding the pad of the finger against the grain, perhaps finding a sensation that it could comprehend.

It stroked the table several more times. Irréelle leaned a tiny bit closer. A floorboard creaked.

Then all at once the Hand rose to the tips of its fingers. It reminded her of a spider seeking its prey (a rather large spider, no doubt, and one with five legs instead of eight, but just as creepy). It crawled to the very edge of the table. When the first finger touched air instead of wood, it paused.

But not for long.

The Hand sprang forward. It landed with a thud upon the floor and shot out with unexpected speed, nimble and light, and aimed straight for Irréelle. She scampered away from it. She was not frightened of it, exactly; only she did not want it to touch her, as if it planned to snatch her body for itself.

"Stop," she said, hoping it would take a command from her the way it had from Miss Vesper. It continued to advance. "Stay," she tried, with no better luck.

The Hand stalked her.

She tried to hop out of its way, but it changed course when she did, drawing all the closer. It was almost on top of her. She stumbled backward. Her elbows banged against the cabinet behind her. The racks and the vials within them rattled and clanked, but somehow they did not fall.

Miss Vesper, who had simply been watching this interaction the way one might observe a cat chasing a mouse, now hurried forward. Her eyebrows pinched together. "Careful."

The Hand sidled closer. Irréelle was cornered.

It made a grab for her ankles, but she kicked it away. Not hard, just enough to keep it from getting hold of her.

The Hand crouched low, poised to jump, and then pushed off from the floor. It smacked into her arm before she could move out of the way. It grabbed at her with searching fingers, snatching the ends of her hair and tugging at the sleeve of her dress. She squirmed and shook until it lost its grip and slid down her side. Instead of falling to the floor, it managed to catch hold of her skirt. It clung to the hem and began to inch upward again.

Frantic, she slapped at the Hand and pried at its fingers. Anything to get it away from her.

"Careful," Miss Vesper said again, her voice an octave higher.

Although Irréelle heard the warning, she was single-minded in her actions and took little care as she swatted at the Hand. "Get off! Get off!" she cried. She yanked the Hand from her skirt and flung it to the ground, but it only popped right back up to the tips of its fingers and angled for another attack.

She lifted the broom just as Miss Vesper said, "Be still."

Instantly, the Hand stopped moving, gone limp in the blink of an eye, but Irréelle was already bringing down the broom. It landed with a crunch and a snap. Bones cracked. She pulled back the broom. The Hand lay broken on the floor.

"How dare you. How *dare* you." Miss Vesper stood stock-still, arms straight at her sides, hands clenched. She never raised her voice, and this time was no exception. If anything, it only grew softer.

Irréelle knew she had made a mistake, one she could not take back, but it was the complete calm in Miss Vesper's voice that told her this mistake was much worse than all her other misbehaviors combined. She might have been forgiven when Irréelle was too slow coming back from the tunnels or when she was forgetful of her tasks. Perhaps her clumsiness and crooked bones could be excused. But not this offense.

She looked up into Miss Vesper's eyes. The blue irises frosted over like ice across a dark lake. Heat bloomed pink on both cheeks. "I did not mean to smash it," Irréelle said. She had only wanted to stop it.

She dropped the broom and sank to her knees. No longer afraid of it, she lifted the Hand, so small like her own. It probably weighed less than a pound. She did not know how she had thought it could have hurt her. Its nails (so very newly grown) were not even long enough to scratch her.

"Your intentions mean little when your actions are so careless. It is why I have never trusted you with what I need most. You would expose yourself and your unnatural form. You would bring unwanted attention to *me*. I cannot let that happen. Little use you have been to me." Miss Vesper twisted the ring on her finger.

The words would have crushed Irréelle if she did not accept them so completely.

She prodded the Hand with one finger, but it lay there motionless. "Is it dead?" She could not bear the thought that she might have killed it. She would not even harm a bug.

"How silly you are. It was never alive," Miss Vesper said. She plucked the Hand from Irréelle's palm and carried it back to the silver tray, tossing it down none too gently. "It was never real. Just a temporary pile of bone dust and imagination."

Only yesterday, Miss Vesper had all but said the exact same thing about Irréelle. She wondered if there was a word that had once woken her, brought her from the dark and the nothing into being. If so, then perhaps there was also a word that would collapse her bones, steal the thoughts from her mind, and extinguish her very existence.

"Like me." She had not meant to speak the thought aloud.

"Exactly like you. Though you are considerably more destructive."

"I'm sorry. Truly and deeply."

"That may be, but you have taken things too far, Irréelle. Sometimes, it is *not* enough that you try so very hard to please me. I am most displeased." Her shoulders went rigid, her features sharpened. She looked less like Miss Vesper and more like a stranger, still pretty and fair, and at the same time not.

Yet hearing her name spoken aloud gave Irréelle some hope, even if the rest of the words hit her painfully. She clambered to her feet. "I will do better. After all, you have kept me all this time."

"I have not been keeping you. What a ridiculous thought. No, you are simply still here until I create another to replace you." The words came out clipped between the tight lines of her mouth. "Which now must be sooner than I had planned."

Irréelle felt all the blood drain from her face. She swayed on her feet, so light-headed her vision blurred, dark at the edges, like she was back in the underside of the graveyard.

"I—" Irréelle began, but Miss Vesper spoke over her.

"You are too troublesome. I find it distasteful to look at you." However, she kept her cold eyes on Irréelle as she lowered her voice and said, quite determined and decided, "I am done with you. I will cut the tether. I will burn your bones. You will be no more."

7

Candlewicks, Firewood, and Bone

Irréelle shuddered. Each word pierced her, just as sharp as any blade. She felt her heart constrict. Erratic as it was, she did not know how it still managed to beat.

I am not a real girl, thought Irréelle. *I am only a girl of dust and bone. It should not matter what becomes of me.* But she could not convince herself of this last point, because it mattered to her very much. More than anything she wanted to be real, and she had ruined any chance of Miss Vesper making her so.

Oh, but she was dizzy. No need to spin in circles for the world to tilt. Round or not, she was about to fall off the very edge.

"Please," she said. "Miss Vesper, please wait."

Miss Vesper ignored her plea. She clasped her hand on Irréelle's arm and dragged her to the attic door. The grip was firm and Irréelle could not pull away, though she did not try very hard, not allowing herself to believe Miss Vesper could actually mean what she had said. She must only be trying to teach Irréelle a lesson.

Down, down, down the spiral staircase they went, faster than she would have liked when she was already so dizzy. She lost her footing, sliding instead of stepping. Thoughts of the careless girl who spilled down the stairs and snapped her neck flashed by. Grasping the railing, she regained her balance on the next step.

Miss Vesper seemed not to notice, but she did slow near the bottom, as if she too might have been thinking of that long-dead girl. Her heels clicked as they always did, an almost reassuring sound. Irréelle could barely keep up. She tripped again and stumbled right into the very straight back of Miss Vesper, who neither slowed nor misstepped, and only continued to pull Irréelle along. It felt like her arm would be ripped from its socket.

She could not keep a straight thought in her head. All she could think of was the chill of Miss Vesper's hand on her arm. Icicles for fingers. As if Miss Vesper's blood ran cold.

They passed by the study and through the dining room and into the kitchen. One-handed, Miss Vesper rummaged through the drawers. She opened one without closing another (the disorganization and haste was most unlike her), and pawed through silverware and wooden spoons and all the other utensils she never used, until she found what she was looking for.

Her fingers closed around a book of matches.

Irréelle shook at the sight of it. "What are those for?"

"They are for lighting fires," Miss Vesper said. "They are for burning things, such as candlewicks, firewood . . . and bones."

"You cannot really mean to . . ." Irréelle choked on the rest of the words.

"Oh yes. I can," said Miss Vesper. She lit a candle left out on the counter and tucked the matchbook away in one of the little pockets of her black dress. "Take it."

Irréelle lifted the candle and Miss Vesper dragged her forward once more, back into the hall and through the door into the basement. The door closed, and Irréelle heard the old tarnished key that always rested unused in the keyhole turn in the lock. And then they were going down the last flight of stairs, into the cold, into the dark, into the basement.

Never before had Irréelle been frightened of the basement or the dark. It was a place like any other. In fact, it was one of the places *most* familiar to her. She did not mind the dusty corners or the cobwebs or the old-potato smell. Of course, it was not as warm or as cozy as the study, with those down-filled armchairs before the fireplace and the fresh lilac air breezing through the open windows, but she knew she did not quite belong in a room so nice as that.

However, as they descended into the basement, she began to tremble.

"Miss Vesper," said Irréelle. Her voice was muffled in the enclosed space. "I have learned my lesson well enough. Please let me help you with the other task. I will stay out of sight. No one will know I am yours."

Miss Vesper took the last three steps in quick succession, almost skipping down them. She turned on Irréelle, pinching her arm between tight fingers as she did so. With Irréelle still on the steps, they stood almost eye level to each other. The candle's flame flickered between them.

Miss Vesper placed her hand to her chest, right over her heart. "Listen to me one last time. You would draw all the neighbors' suspicious eyes to my door. I will not allow it. If anyone were to see you lurching through the graveyard, they would think they had seen a ghost." She yanked Irréelle down the last few steps. "Or worse. No one should ever set their eyes upon you."

She pushed Irréelle ahead of her. "Sit," she said, shoving Irréelle down onto a crate of potatoes.

Hot wax dripped onto Irréelle's hand. It stung for a second, but dried so quickly on her skin the pain was gone the very next second. She thought it would hurt much worse, that the wax would sink into her bones and begin to burn them, just as Miss Vesper was threatening to do.

Although she wanted to deny it, it was beginning to sink in that Miss Vesper was entirely serious. Irréelle's heart tightened up into a little ball, and she wanted to curl up around it, protecting it.

Miss Vesper walked into the shadows. "Now where is the kerosene?"

Irréelle's head snapped up. She gripped the rough edge of the crate beneath her. Her mind raced. She needed a plan, but every idea that came to mind she discarded. She could not run back up the stairs because Miss Vesper had locked the door and hidden the key in her pocket. She could not snuff out the flame because Miss Vesper would only light it again. She had not even the broom to defend herself.

And then, when she had almost lost hope, she knew what she had to do.

She took a deep breath to gather herself. Then she slowly stood up, careful not to make a sound or tip the crate and send the potatoes rolling. She set down the candle so Miss Vesper would not notice the light flickering from one place to another.

Miss Vesper moved boxes here to there, rattling cans and shifting crates as she searched the shelves for the tin of oil. The noise covered the sounds of Irréelle's creaking bones and her footsteps across the floor.

She touched her hands to the brick wall, but they were shaking so badly, and she kept looking back over her shoulder, so it took her longer than it should have to find those indentations in the wall. When at last her fingers latched on, she pressed down with all her might, and the door to the tunnels swung open with a whoosh of stale air.

The passageway was as black as night.

At the same time she went for the candle, Miss Vesper turned to face her. Irréelle did not hesitate. She swiped the candle up in one hand and darted for the door. But she had gone no more than a few steps when a terrible tugging (so very different from the pull of the bones) drew her backward.

"Come," Miss Vesper said.

Though she strained to go forward, Irréelle shuffled back another step. It was frightening, to be commanded by the very thread that connected her to Miss Vesper. Irréelle struggled against it, leaning toward the door. She had never felt so small, so insignificant, in all her life.

"*Come*," Miss Vesper demanded.

Irréelle's feet betrayed her again, but she still had control of her hands. When she came even with the crate, she gave it a great shove. As the crate toppled, potatoes tumbled to the ground. Miss Vesper leapt out of the way. Her focus faltered. The tugging sensation melted away, and Irréelle raced for the door.

"Where do you think you are going?" Miss Vesper called out, her voice fatigued. "You know there is no way out."

Anywhere else, Irréelle thought, though it broke her heart, for she loved Miss Vesper even then. She did not want to, but the feeling was not one she could shake loose, for it was settled deep in her bones.

Candle in hand, she shut the door, leaving Miss Vesper in absolute darkness. Something heavy thudded against the wall from the other side. She thought she heard Miss Vesper shout her name, but it sounded very far away through the earth and bricks, so she could not be sure.

She did not wait to see if Miss Vesper would follow her into the passageway. Irréelle ran.

8

The Midnight Creatures

She had never run so fast in her life or been so light on her feet. It almost felt as if she were someone else. Someone who did not let crooked bones or fear slow her. Someone who defied orders and made her own choices. Each footfall, though not altogether quiet, was purposeful. She flew down the passageway, white hair streaming behind her.

The candle's flame fluttered. Shadows bounced across the walls.

Irréelle slowed and stole a glance over her shoulder. Nothing but darkness. She listened for any sound other than her breathing.

From the gloom came the groan of the hidden door.

Irréelle backed away. She could not pull her eyes from the pocket of darkness. Within it, the smallest flame sparked to life. Miss Vesper had struck a match. It hovered there a moment, glowing red, and then dropped through the air, touching oil as it landed.

All at once the light swelled and then snaked closer, a line of fire along the wall. It burned in the metal trough, chasing after Irréelle.

At the far end of the passageway, Miss Vesper stood in the doorway, a slim silhouette. The flames leapt, throwing shadows and light upon her face. Her eyes glittered orange, reflecting the fire.

She glared at Irréelle but made no move to come after her. Not even the tips of her shoes entered the tunnel, as if Miss Vesper could not bear the confinement. Holding very still, she lifted her hand.

Irréelle tensed, expecting her feet to listen to some instruction from Miss Vesper and march her back to the basement, but they continued to follow Irréelle's wishes. Although something tugged in her belly, the distance between them must have been too great for Miss Vesper to overcome. But there was little time to savor the moment.

Around them, the walls trembled. Irréelle stumbled as dirt broke off in great chunks from the ceiling. It clumped together in midair, shifting and pulsing, as if it *breathed* in sync with Miss Vesper's temper.

With a twist of her wrist, another tremor shook the tunnel. The dirt scattered and re-formed into familiar shapes—the creatures of the night Irréelle was used to seeing hanging upside down from the eaves of the house. Only these earth-forged bats were misshapen things, with lumpy bodies and terrible, pointed ears.

They glowered at Irréelle with empty eye sockets and gnashed their ugly dirt-made teeth. Miss Vesper pointed one long finger at Irréelle. In a black cloud, the bats flew down the tunnel, so many of them they blotted out the figure of Miss Vesper.

Irréelle shrieked, staggering toward the other passageways even though she knew no way out of them. Always she had returned to Miss Vesper after collecting bone dust. The thought of escape had never crossed her mind in the past, but it spurred her on now.

One more backward glance confirmed the bats were gaining on her unimpressive lead. They flew as if they had always known how to do so.

Irréelle lumbered forward as if she still had not mastered her form. Her legs pumped an awkward rhythm. Her breath hitched. She ran until she thought her lungs would burst with all their wheezing, but she could not outrun Miss Vesper's monstrous bats.

Their oversized shadows reached her first. She flinched, as if something immaterial might still be able to touch her.

Then the bats swooped closer. Their wings beat the air, a lacework of dirt and cobwebs. They brushed past her cheeks and darted between her ankles. Irréelle recoiled, losing her footing. Her shoulder slammed into the wall and a sharp pain shot down her arm. But she did not fall.

She clutched the candle tight, protecting the flame as best she could while swatting at the bats with her other hand. They crumbled when she struck them. Dirt spattered her face.

But they kept coming, tiny claws pinching, as if Miss Vesper meant for them to snatch her by the arms and drag her back to the basement.

Irréelle would not let them. She had come this far already, striking out on her own, and the free-fall feeling of escape rushed through her.

The glow of her candlelight danced across the entrance to the diverging passageways just ahead. She charged forward, elbowing the bats flying close by her side and knocking the creatures from the air. They fell soundless beneath her boots. She darted into the closest passageway and took the first turn. The rest of the bats followed, although some were not as swift as others and crashed into the walls, scattering dirt as they broke apart.

They did not know the tunnels the way Irréelle did, how sharp the turns, where the ceiling lowered, the smaller paths leading from one passageway to the next. And they were moving too quickly, so eager to catch her that some flew right past as she took another turn and then another.

Her feet led her deeper, toward the tunnels that wound and twisted beneath the oldest part of the graveyard. Here, her favorite skeletons rested, and though she hated to disturb them, Irréelle felt safer the nearer she came to the hum of their bones, as if they would watch over her and ward off Miss Vesper's bats. Though the bones thrummed kindly at her heartstrings, they could not slow its over-fast beating.

Something cold and crumbly touched her neck. A bat sneaking closer and the whisper of its wing. Its fangs bared, ready to strike at her throat.

Irréelle batted it away, swallowing a scream as more of them formed, wings and bodies and mouths tearing loose from the ceiling.

She sped up, winding a confusing path farther and farther into the underside of the graveyard. The midnight creatures fought one another for the lead, scratching and clawing and biting their way forward. It slowed them, briefly, and Irréelle stole away, slipping out of view before they rounded the corner.

She took several quick turns. Behind her, the raging of bat wings softened. She could not tell how far behind they had fallen.

Every sound in the dark warned of their approach, or something worse. She told herself it was a lone bat and nothing more. Yet what if it was not a bat? What if Miss Vesper found the courage to enter the tunnel, spreading fire in her wake? Irréelle sniffed the air, but the only smoke came from her candle.

However, fire was not Miss Vesper's only tool. If she grew tired of the chase, she might whisper one word and still Irréelle, just as she had the Hand. Miss Vesper might have thought this all a game, one she could win at any moment.

But it was a cruel game.

Irréelle knew there must be goodness in Miss Vesper, for how could Irréelle love her otherwise? Did a creator not need love to craft its creation? But any glimmer of goodness or love seemed to be locked away, something she was unwilling to share with Irréelle.

Irréelle stopped quite suddenly, caught by the heaviness of her thoughts. She looked left and then right. Each path was equally dark. And each path echoed with the whooshing of bat wings striking air. Though she stood perfectly still, her heart pounded.

She tore around the next corner.

And ran headlong into the army of bats.

Her hand flew up to cover her face, but it was too late. They swooped close, rushing over her body, grabbing at her hair and dress. Her skin prickled wherever they touched her.

"Get off! Let go!" she cried, slapping and squirming as they gripped tighter, dragging her several feet. She dug her heels into the ground and thrust out her arm, smacking several bats into the wall.

The rest fought their way closer. She swatted at the ones clutching her shoulders and kicked at the ones circling her ankles, and at last broke free. Without once looking back, she charged down the nearest tunnel. Her feet clomped. Her legs teetered.

And then the toe of her boot struck something across the path. She stumbled, but caught herself against the wall. A draft blew her hair into her face.

She stood in front of the one archway that she always, *always* avoided.

The whisper came on the breeze. That ghostlike call. It sent chills through her body, like the worst tickle. She started to edge past and away, but then, in the darkness, closer than the beating of the bats' dirt-made wings, she heard rustling.

9

The Whispering Passageway

The rustling drew closer, a scuttling sound that filled the tunnel so Irréelle could not determine from which direction it came. It could be approaching from ahead, and of course, the bats attacked from behind.

The whispering passageway beckoned.

With nowhere else to go, Irréelle squeezed through the archway she had always made a point to avoid. A moment later, the bats shot by in a frantic storm.

But they could circle back at any moment, sniffing her out with whatever strange senses they possessed. She groped her way past the thick tree root and into the partially collapsed tunnel.

The rustling came closer, grew louder. She flattened

herself against the wall and held her breath. From the depths of the tunnel, the draft continued to whisper, like words tangled in a breeze. But she could not focus on that now. Something was just outside the archway, shuffling, sneaking, slowing.

She edged backward, away from the scampering that sounded like a mouse, or maybe something larger, like a rat. One made of dirt and spiderwebs, sent by Miss Vesper to gnaw at her ankles. Irréelle shuddered, pressing into the inky, nightmare black, hoping it hid her completely.

The walls pinched around her, closer and closer the deeper she went.

The whisper came again. Quite close. Quite raspy.

And a hand, most certainly a hand, grabbed her ankle.

She shrieked, tried to twist out of its grasp, but instead lost her balance and fell to her knees. When she hit the ground, she dropped the candle. It rolled out of reach. The wick hissed, and the flame sputtered out.

Irréelle blinked into the absolute darkness.

"Who's there?" she said. Dirt sprinkled down from the ceiling.

Silence.

And then a voice came low and raspy. "Sorry." A cough. "Are you hurt?"

Irréelle scooted forward, away from the rusty-hinge voice. It might be another one of Miss Vesper's creatures, one that spoke softly but had teeth like knives, waiting for her to come close enough so it could snatch her away. Her hands swept the ground. She would find the candle and run, never mind the bats or the rat or whatever it was in the main tunnel.

"Who's there?" she asked again.

"I've been calling to you for such a long time," the voice said softly. "Have you any light? I'm stuck, you see." A laugh, low and scratchy, filled the tiny chamber. "Of course, you can't see. These tunnels are darker than midnight, than a raven's wing, than sleep."

Her hands bumped into the candle, wedged in tight next to a rock. She wrenched it free, and it struck her just then who this disembodied voice might belong to. She whipped around to face the voice in the darkness.

It was a boy's voice gone dry with disuse. Or else hoarse with shouting. "Are you the boy?"

"She called me Boy."

Of course, Irréelle knew exactly whom "she" referred to. Miss Vesper. Irréelle scrambled over to him, found his hand on the ground. He wrapped his fingers around hers. They felt cold.

But not as cold as the shiver raising the hairs on the back of her neck. Like something had followed her into the darkness and crept closer.

"What's that?" she whispered, expecting a swarm of bats to come around the corner at any moment.

The boy did not respond, as if he was listening. The only sound was their breathing.

"I can almost see you," he said, breaking the quiet. "Your hair is very white."

"Shh. Don't let the bats hear you." Irréelle swallowed the panic that tightened her throat and warbled her words.

"Bats are harmless," he said.

"These are not," she said, but if the boy showed no fear, she did not want to announce her own. "I can't see a thing. I have a candle," she said. "But no matches."

"I have matches, but no candle." He pulled his hand away and fumbled in the dark. "They're here somewhere." She heard rustling and again imagined a creature inching closer, but this time it was only the boy placing a matchbox in her palm.

She struck a match, sparking a flame. It glowed orange and red and was so suddenly bright in the pitch-black tunnel that Irréelle, at first, could see nothing beyond the flame.

And then she saw two eyes shining in the dark.

She lit the wick and held the candle up to her face. "I'm Irréelle."

The eyes blinked several times, rapidly. She took in the boy's thin, dirt-streaked face. He squinted as if he were looking at the sun. She did not mean to gape, but it hit her all at once. She had never seen a boy up close before, having only spied them from her window when they walked past the house, and certainly, she had never spoken with a boy before. No matter how silly, she felt suddenly shy.

"I prefer Guy to Boy," he said in his gravelly voice. "Do you think you could give me a hand? As I said, I'm stuck."

"Oh!" Irréelle said. "Of course."

But still she could not move. She stared at the boy, who looked back at her with equal interest. He lay awkwardly on his side, his torso and both legs buried beneath huge piles of dirt and rock. They flattened him to the ground, leaving only his head, shoulders, and arms free. It looked like he grew from the ground itself. He propped himself up on one elbow as best he could. His hair, black and (understandably) unkempt, fell across his forehead.

"I'm sorry." Irréelle continued to stare. "I'm so sorry I did not find you sooner." She did not want to admit all the times she had passed by the tunnel, but she found herself saying, quite honestly, "I heard the whispers all this time, but was too frightened to follow them."

He attempted to shrug. Dirt fell from his shoulders to the ground. "You're here now."

"Yes. Yes, I am."

She set the candle down on a low ledge. The flame, though small, filled the chamber with soft light. When she stood, she realized just how tiny the space was in which she found herself, and in which the boy must have been trapped for such a long time.

From the corner of her eye, she saw something scamper by in the shadows. She spun toward it. "Did you see it this time?"

Guy frowned. "Maybe."

"Then let's hurry." She returned to his side.

"That rock there." He pointed. "Start with that one, if you could."

Squatting low and pressing the heels of her boots into the ground, she wedged her shoulder against a heavy rock and leaned into it with the weight of her body. She jostled and strained until, at last, it rolled aside.

Beneath, she saw the tip of his boot. The next rock, although smaller, took longer to move. It was flat and wide and sunken in the dirt. She heaved and tugged, shoved and grunted, and then she pulled with all her might and the rock dislodged. It just missed dropping on her toes as she stumbled backward.

Guy's boot shifted. "I can move my foot!"

"What happened to you down here?" Irréelle swiped her hair from her eyes and looked around the small chamber, not at all sure the dirt walls would continue to hold. Not at all sure what might be sneaking closer when her back was turned.

"One moment I was walking through the tunnel and the next moment, it collapsed on top of me."

"How awful," she said, working faster. "How long have you been stuck here?" She slid her fingers beneath a large gray rock and edged it inch by inch off his leg.

"Months, I'm sure."

"How is that possible?"

"I have no idea," he said. "Perhaps I'm a ghost."

"Perhaps you're a ghost." In the habit of agreeing with whatever Miss Vesper said, she repeated his words automatically, but then she shook her head. "Well, no. That's just silly. You are not a ghost."

"Of course I'm not." He squirmed a bit, but was not yet able to maneuver his legs out from under the rocks.

The stones shifted and exposed his other boot.

She was not used to his raspy voice. He almost did sound like a ghoul in the dark, haunting her. She considered, working another rock loose. "It must be the bone dust."

"That makes more sense," he said. "And the worms."

"Worms?"

"I had to eat something, didn't I?"

"I suppose you did." But her stomach flipped at the thought. Although she had not eaten for hours and hours, the thought of slimy, dirt-covered worms squiggling down her throat quite relieved her of hunger.

"No crickets this deep down, so worms it was."

As she did not want to offend the first boy she had met by telling him eating bugs was disgusting, she merely nodded and focused on the rocks. Even more careful now, imagining all the insects she might uncover.

Stone by stone, Irréelle unburied him. Every few seconds she craned her neck, searching the candlelit chamber for signs of Miss Vesper's twisted creations. She could not shake the feeling that they were being *watched*.

She dug faster, until he was free, and then stepped back to give him space. "Are you able to stand?"

Guy looked up at her. A too-wide grin spread across

his face, revealing a chipped front tooth. His boots moved, just a little, as if he were wiggling his toes. He rotated one ankle, and then another. He bent his knees, and they made a horrible cracking sound that seemed not to bother him at all. His bones creaked as he pushed himself to standing.

He took one hesitant step, and then he lunged for Irréelle.

IO

The Good-for-Almost-Nothing Boy

She raised her arms in front of her face. Not that it did much good.

He staggered forward with hands outstretched and grabbed her shoulders. The force sent her stumbling backward, right into the wall. Stones pressed into her crooked spine. A spattering of dirt rained onto the tops of their heads.

His face hovered only inches from hers, hair in his gray eyes, grime on his cheeks, and a snarl on his lips. He did not smell the best either. Irréelle turned her head to the side and tried to hold him at arm's length.

She pushed against his chest. Just once. Not even that hard.

Startled, his hands slid from her shoulders. He had not, she realized, been holding very tightly, which likely meant he had not lunged at her either, and instead, being so unused to standing, had simply fallen toward her. As if to confirm this observation, he tottered on his feet, flailed his arms about, and, with nothing to support him, fell heavily to the ground.

He groaned on impact. His legs stuck out straight in front of him, and he glared at them.

"I'm afraid I'm not very steady yet," he said. "My legs are all pins and needles." He thumped his thighs as if to get some feeling back into them.

"Oh my." Irréelle knelt beside him. Her cheeks warmed. "I'm sorry. Let me help you."

"I think I've got it," he said.

She took hold of his arm anyway and hoisted him to his feet. He rocked back and forth on his heels, shifted his weight from one foot to the other, and grinned wider than she had thus far seen.

Standing beside him, she realized he was quite a bit taller than her, but just as skinny. (With only worms to eat, she would have all but wasted away, she was sure.) His shirt was dirty and spotted with holes. The sleeves exposed bony wrists. Dirt and dust caked his too-short pants. She could see the tops of his boots, and those too were scuffed and worn.

He looked down at himself. "I think I've grown." He held out his arms and turned them this way and that.

"Maybe you've been down here longer than you thought. How old were you then?"

"I'm not sure," he said. "I've never known my age. But I remember Miss Vesper saying I looked like a good-for-almost-nothing boy approximately a decade old. How old do I look to you now?" He lifted his chin and turned his head from side to side for her to better judge his age.

Irréelle thought about the question and looked at him quite seriously. "Well," she said, "a decade plus one- or two-tenths of a decade, I would say."

He became quiet then. He pulled on his sleeve, but it went no lower on his arm. "I guess that must be right, then."

"It's as good an age as any." She wanted to reassure him, to make him feel better, but she was not sure of the right thing to say.

"Let's get out of here already," he said, sounding a little defeated that so much time might have passed.

"Yes, let's," Irréelle agreed, ear tuned to the sounds in the dark. Something burrowed through the dirt and rocks. "Can you manage on your own?"

"Course I can." His voice came out as a rather loud croak.

"Quiet," Irréelle warned. Her eyes darted toward the entrance to the tunnel. "I'm hiding."

"From the bats?" Guy practiced walking in a straight line.

Already he was better at it than Irréelle, but she pretended not to notice. "Miss Vesper, of course."

"Why would she be looking for *you*?" He kicked at a rock on the ground. It bounced against the wall. Dirt crumbled.

Irréelle did not want to repeat Miss Vesper's threat about burning her bones. It made her heart leap to her throat just thinking of it, but the words she forced out were no better. "She wants to imagine me away." Irréelle could not believe Miss Vesper had not done so already. The threat of it loomed wherever she went, like thunder following lightning.

It struck her then how useless it was to run away when she would always be tethered to Miss Vesper.

Guy stopped walking and turned to look at her. "Why?"

"Doesn't matter," Irréelle said. She crossed her arms, the left tucked beneath the right to hide their uneven lengths.

He shook his head. "Miss Vesper won't come into the tunnels. Her face goes bone-white when she talks of them."

Although Irréelle had never seen Miss Vesper visit the underside of the graveyard, it did not seem Miss Vesper would be frightened of anything. It was one of the things Irréelle most admired about her. "But I heard rustling. You heard it too."

"You heard *something*," he said, and she was grateful he had not dismissed her entirely, "but it was not Miss Vesper."

"How can you be so sure?" Irréelle wanted to believe him.

His eyes darkened. "She never came for me, did she?"

How horrible, thought Irréelle, but she kept her voice light when she said, "Miss Vesper spoke of you highly." That was not exactly true, so she amended, "Or at least, she spoke of you, that is."

And just then, she could not help but wonder if Miss Vesper would forgive her if she brought Guy back to the house with her. Or even if Miss Vesper might imagine her real in reward. After all, Miss Vesper had asked about the boy. She had seemed to trust him with some unknown task she would not assign to Irréelle.

"Didn't you say she thought you were good-for-*almost*-nothing? That basically means you are good-for-*something*.

I think she would be very happy to see you."

Perhaps she had exaggerated this last statement, as nothing seemed to make Miss Vesper happy, and Irréelle felt rather bad about stretching the truth, but oh, she already missed her bedroom and the great fireplace in the study and the scent of lilacs. And yes, as much as she did not want to, she missed Miss Vesper too.

Or at least the idea of her. Someone who might accept Irréelle as she was, who might love her and care for her, despite all her imperfections.

Guy was not listening. He kicked another stone, this one larger than the last. It struck the wall like a thunderclap, and cracks spread through the dirt like dark lines of lightning.

"What's happening?" Irréelle asked. She raised a shaky hand to the wall. A vibration coursed through her palm and up her arm.

Guy stood perfectly still. Beneath the dirt, his face went white. "Don't move."

Irréelle could not have moved even if she had wanted to, as she was frozen with fright.

Within the walls, soil and stones shifted and groaned. Dirt fell in chunks from the ceiling into their hair, into their eyes. A draft leaked through the tunnel as if thrust out from the fractures in the earth. From above, from below, the ground quaked.

One breath of silence followed. Irréelle blinked dirt from her eyes. Guy coughed.

And then the ceiling collapsed upon them.

II

The Hollow

It lasted only seconds, the grinding, shifting earth, the falling dirt and rock. Irréelle threw her arms over her head and huddled on the ground. She kept her face down, her eyes closed. Her breaths came very fast.

One last sprinkling of dirt, and the earth settled once more. She was afraid to move, afraid to disturb the sudden quiet. But slowly, she lifted her head. She lowered her arms. Dirt fell down the collar of her dress and clung to her eyelashes. She brushed it away.

She was neither buried nor harmed. She was safe.

Ahead of her, a narrow tunnel cut a slit into the earth, the opening revealed only when the ceiling caved in. A draft blew against her cheeks.

"Guy, look," she said. "Guy," she called again, louder this time when he did not immediately reply.

A low moan rasped from a dry throat. "I'm here, Irréelle." Rocks rolled to the side. Guy sat up, shaking dirt from his hair.

Somehow the candle still burned, and in its warm glow Irréelle smiled. "Do you see?"

"Oh yes, I see." Guy crawled backward, fast-like, his eyes focused not on the unearthed tunnel but on a dark crevice just in front of him.

Within, something rustled. Not bat wings whooshing, not rocks shifting, not dirt crumbling. No, whatever it was, it scuttled. The same sound she had heard chasing after her in the main passageway and sneaking around the chamber out of sight.

It crept from the crevice beneath the rocks.

It was not a dirt-made rat, as she had expected. No, it was much worse.

It was the Hand.

Slim fingers emerged one at a time until all of them were visible and tapping. The Hand squatted in the shadows and then dashed forward. Two of the fingers were still bent, though the breaks appeared mended, and the injury did not seem to slow it. It maneuvered over the dirt like a spider.

"What's that?" Guy scrambled to his feet.

He had been in the dark so long, he must have thought his eyes were playing tricks on him. "I'm afraid it's a dust-and-bone hand."

It scurried toward them.

"Stay," Irréelle said. "Stop. Freeze. Hold still." She tried to remember how Miss Vesper had halted its progression. She closed her eyes, visualized Miss Vesper, imagined her voice. "Be still!" she cried, eyes opening once more.

Of course, it did not heed her command. Miss Vesper was its creator, just as she was Irréelle's creator.

The Hand charged forward and then broke to the left. As quick as could be, it snatched the candle from the ledge and began dragging it away.

"Stop it!" Irréelle said.

Guy was already moving forward and she followed after. The Hand sped up. It wove between their feet as if it meant to trip them. It darted out of reach when they grabbed for it. At the same time as Irréelle, Guy lunged for the Hand, and they collided. Heads knocked together, limbs entwined. Their bodies thumped to the ground.

The Hand raced toward the drafty tunnel and then it was gone, the candle with it.

The light dimmed. Shadows crept closer.

Without the candle, they might never find their way from the underside of the graveyard. Although Irréelle knew the ins and outs of the tunnels, she could not imagine navigating them in complete darkness. Already, it pressed her tight, a suffocating constriction in her chest. She wondered if this slip of terror was a feeling Miss Vesper knew as well and the reason she kept far from the passages.

"Come on!" Guy clambered to his feet and pulled Irréelle up with him.

She darted ahead. They chased the dimming light into the narrowest of passageways. Everything around them, shadows and gloom.

Except Irréelle thought she caught sight of a heart carved into the dirt wall as she raced past. A silly imagining, to be sure, and one she would have dismissed, but a few feet later she spied another one, just visible in the wavering light.

Wherever was the Hand leading them?

She and Guy charged after it, through the heart-lined tunnel. "Do you think someone marked the way out?" Irréelle asked.

"Those are hearts, not arrows," Guy huffed, winded from running.

She let his words bounce off her back, clinging to

hope, and at last they entered another chamber, one larger than all the others. However, Irréelle stopped very suddenly (and Guy stumbled right into her), for she could immediately see all four walls were solid stone and dirt.

There was no sign of the Hand, though the candle rested in the dirt near her feet, shining directly upon the large, heavy object before them.

The flame flickered, illuminating an open casket. She was quite used to seeing caskets in the underside of the graveyard, so she barely noticed its presence at first. Instead, she snatched the candle from the ground and her eyes scanned the chamber in search of some small passageway she might have overlooked. That draft had come from *somewhere* and the hearts must lead to *something*.

"It's a dead end," she whispered.

Guy pushed past her. "There has to be a way out." He circled the chamber once and then again.

Irréelle leaned against the wall, keeping out of Guy's way as he circled a third time. When he passed by, his gray eyes flashed silver. He prowled like a wild animal locked in a cage, half-starved, half-mad, and desperate for escape.

And then all at once he stopped. His head snapped to the side. "The casket," he said. Something within it had captured his attention.

She brought the candle to Guy's side and gasped when the light fell upon the casket. They stared at it openmouthed. It had a dark wood exterior, the edges carved with a design of leaves and flowers, and a pleated black interior of what looked like the finest satin, even under a layer of dust.

"It's empty," he said.

Irréelle looked over her shoulder as if the missing skeleton might have sneaked up behind her, but of course nothing was there but her own shadow on the wall. "But how? Where are the bones?" Her mind spun with ideas but settled on only one. She shivered. "Could the Hand have taken them?" She listened for its scampering, but still heard nothing.

"It could have. It was fast. It could have stolen the bones if it took them one by one." He wiggled his fingers. "But probably not. I think they were gone before we got here."

Just the thought of the missing bones sent goose bumps across her skin. Along with the musty air and the dark corners even the candlelight would not reveal, it felt different from the other nooks in the underside that she had previously visited.

The trunk of a tree took up the far wall. The bark crackled with disease. Roots broke through the dirt, straggly ones that hung from the ceiling just as they did in the other tunnels, except here they were dark and twisted and dry as bone. One had wrapped itself around the edge of the casket, splitting the wood as it spread across the ruffled pillow.

Guy swung toward Irréelle and plucked the candle from her hand. His hair hung across his forehead, disheveled and dirty. Though he had not touched it, it blew into his eyes. The draft tousled Irréelle's hair too, and tickled the back of her neck.

"Do you feel that?" She held up her hand, trying to gauge the direction of the breeze.

"It's just the ghosts," he said. "They're always roaming."

With the empty casket beside her and the cemetery above her, she could almost believe in ghosts, but she shook her head. "No, the draft has to be coming from somewhere."

He frowned. "Where?" He swung the candle around, and as he did, it swept near the trunk of the tree.

"Turn around," Irréelle said, excitement bubbling. "Turn around."

Guy faced the tree trunk, candle aloft. Firelight fell through the decaying bark. "It's hollow." He spun in a circle. "It's hollow! We'll climb our way out." He whooped and turned, stumbling all around the chamber in celebration.

A draft swooped down from above and trickled through the lattice of rot. Irréelle touched the bark. It was dry in places and slick with mold in others, and it left her fingertips black. She began to peel the bark away. It was thicker than she expected and broke her nails as she scratched against it.

"Help me," she said.

But Guy spun past her, limbs jerky like a puppet on the end of its strings. He looked entirely silly, his wide smile glowing in the firelight.

"Come on," he said, and took her filthy hand in his filthier one.

"Not now," she said, but he turned her in a circle. Once she started, she found she did not want to stop. Her white hair flew around her shoulders. Sparks spit up from the candle in his hand, like stars streaking across a black sky. They spun and spun, and their shadows spun with them.

They laughed, and since neither of them had much occasion to smile, the unpracticed sound was disjointed and rough-edged, and all the more delightful because of its purity. It echoed around them.

Irréelle became so dizzy her feet tangled together. Only then did she slow, catching herself against the dirt wall, and only then, out of breath and the world atilt, did she think of the pigtailed girls at play. She could not believe she had spun, like they had, with such abandon.

Finally, Guy stopped his spinning as well. He staggered over to her and pushed back a lock of black hair that had fallen into his eyes. "What are we waiting for?" He grinned, as if she had been the one to grab his hand.

"Not a thing," she said.

The oak groaned as they tore into it with their bare hands.

12

The Above Side of the Graveyard

Side by side they worked. They said not a word and focused solely on carving a hole in the tree. The dead wood splintered. The wind found the tiniest cracks in the old tree and whined down the hollow.

They did not stop until they had gouged a hole in the trunk wide enough to fit through. "You should go first," Irréelle said. "After all, you've been down here much longer than I have."

His eyes clouded over. He took a deep sigh and stepped into the hollow, his silhouette outlined in orange flame.

"Hold this for me." He thrust the candle toward Irréelle.

She crept into the tree beside him. There was just

enough room for them both at the base, but the tree grew narrower as it rose.

As Guy began to climb, black flecks of wood dusted down, scuffed off by his boots. Irréelle continued to look upward anyway and shielded her eyes with her hand as best she could. "Hurry," she said, and then imagined him tumbling down the hollow and added, "but be careful."

His hand slipped and then caught. "I'm always careful." His scratchy voice floated down to her.

She thought of him trapped in the tunnel and was not reassured. "Be *more* careful."

Soon after, she heard the crunch of dry wood breaking. It fell in larger pieces than before and she ducked her head. *We'll soon be out*, she thought, too superstitious to say the words aloud.

"Watch out," he said from above.

Irréelle stepped back into the chamber just as debris fell down the hollow and hit the ground where she had been standing. Along with it fell a shaft of frail light.

"Come on!" Guy called. "Come up!"

She blew out the candle and then rushed into the hollow. Her fingertips were sore and full of slivers, but she reached out and took hold of the first notch she could find. Scaling the tree, she might suffer a hundred more slivers, but she would be glad to have them if only she could make it to the top.

A fourth of the way up, her fingers curled around a knot that was damp to the touch. As she pulled upward it gave way. The rot crumbled. Her hand searched for another grip, flailing until it caught hold of a rough outcropping. She clung to the tree, pressed her face right to the wood, and did not move until she regained her balance. Not once did she look down.

As she neared the top, Irréelle thought she felt something brush against her ankle and scamper up her leg, but the sensation was gone as quickly as it had come. Likely just a trick of the wind.

Fractured light poured through the opening above. She focused on that until her hand reached through the hole and grabbed hold of a raised root. She squirreled out of the tree and knelt in the grass. It stained her knees green. Behind her, the dead tree sprouted black and twisted from the earth. Long branches, dripping with moss, stretched overhead and reached for the darkening sky.

She pushed to her feet.

For the first time, atop a small hill, Irréelle stood in the above side of the graveyard. It must have mirrored the tunnels below, but she felt lost among the long stretches of grass and the meandering pathways. The gray headstones lined in perfect rows gave it a somber tone. Angels wept into their hands. Gargoyles crouched with folded wings. It was all strangely beautiful in the pre-dusk evening.

The light was more silver than gold, misty, as if it might rain. It filtered through the branches and warmed her skin and seeped into her bones. She tilted her face toward the setting sun and let it chase the chills away. All this fresh air, she sucked it into her lungs. It smelled of grass and cherry blossoms.

She peeked at Guy from the corner of her eye, giving him space to take everything in. He squinted, but seemed set on staring straight at the sun, though his eyes must have burned. His chest rose and fell as if he struggled to catch his breath.

In the light, she saw more than the dust across his face and the dirt caked in his hair. He looked strong and fragile all at once. His jaw was set in a firm, straight line, and his eyes were dark and glassy.

They stood there, in the cover of the dead oak, and watched the sun sink beneath the horizon. Above them, the sky dimpled with the first stars of the night. The gravestones turned white in the moonlight.

"It looks like I chased the sun away," Guy said.

"Or maybe you just called to the moon." Irréelle walked toward him.

"Are you hurt? You're limping."

"I'm fine." She gave him a closed-mouth smile that was not really a smile at all.

"Okay," Guy said. "Well, anyway . . . thanks. I thought I was going to be stuck in the tunnel forever, and that's a very long time indeed."

"I'm glad I found you," she replied.

"Now, if only you had brought a hot bath and a hot meal along with you, it would have been a proper rescue." He brushed his hands over his sleeves. Dirt fell from the folds and wrinkles.

"If only." Of course, then it was all she could think about. Soaking in a tub full of bubbles, water so hot it turned her skin pink and eased the aches from her bones, followed by a potato potpie warm from the oven. Her stomach rumbled.

She wanted to return to the house at once. If she arrived with Guy, Miss Vesper would have to see she was useful, able to find someone who was missing for so long. Maybe she would trust her with the other task, whatever it might be. And maybe they could build a different relationship, the kind Irréelle had always longed for.

But as it was, Miss Vesper would take one look at them, one whiff of them, and follow through on her threat to imagine Irréelle away and burn her bones. She could not let that happen.

"We can't present ourselves to Miss Vesper looking like this," she said, and slapped her hands against her thighs. Dust rose from her skirt.

"I thought you ran away from her." Guy poked his finger through a hole in his trousers, which only made it bigger.

"Yes, well, I shouldn't have done so. I could never outrun Miss Vesper's reach anyway." She tensed, fearful that Miss Vesper might strike her down then and there, patience waning, at last returning Irréelle to dust for her disobedience. "It all might have been a misunderstanding. She's probably as worried about me as she is about you." Irréelle crossed her arms, cradling the left one against her stomach, dismayed by how false her words sounded. So wistful for the way things *could* have been.

He raised his eyebrow. "I suppose that's true. She's equally not worried about either one of us."

"Oh, that's a horrible thing to say." Irréelle frowned at the truth in his words, but pressed on. "You see, she will have to forgive me when I bring you back with me."

Forgive me and accept me.

Guy shook his head. "I doubt that." His hoarse voice came out as a whisper. "Besides, I'm never going back."

13

Night Folds Close

She wanted to throttle him.

Her hands fell to her sides and she clenched her skirt in tight fists so he would not see them shaking. The wind whined through the branches as if in harmony with her dark mood and lashed her hair into her face. Irréelle did not bother to brush it away. "But you have to. You have to come back with me."

"I'm not," Guy said. "There's no way. Not ever." He clenched his jaw, which looked especially sharp on his long, thin face.

"But Miss Vesper needs us." Her throat tightened up. She imagined Miss Vesper sitting in the armchair before the fireplace, alone with her insomnia, staring into the dying embers as she paged through her tiny notebook. Waiting for her sleeping serum to heavy her eyelids.

But if Irréelle was honest, it was not Miss Vesper who needed them, but Irréelle who needed Miss Vesper.

She sighed, already knowing he would not like the next thing she would say, but it weighed on her more than anything. "It's the only thing I can think of to earn her forgiveness."

"What do you want to go back there for?" His gravelly voice sounded more abrasive than its usual rasp. "Why do you want her forgiveness?"

Irréelle lifted her head. She looked straight at him with her muddled eyes, one green and gold and brown, the other flecked with blue. She did not fold her arms to hide their uneven lengths or straighten her shoulders to affect better posture. She knew he could not help but see her white hair and pale lashes, and every bony, crooked angle of her body. "I don't belong anywhere else."

This time, he was the one to look away. "Don't say that," he mumbled.

"Well, it's true, isn't it?" She wanted him to admit it as much as she wanted him to deny it, but of course she could not have it both ways.

"I don't know where you belong," he said. She lifted her chin, but he was not finished. "But you do not belong with Miss Vesper."

"Then I don't belong *anywhere*. I am not even real." The words slipped out, the deepest, most awful fear she kept close to her heart, affirmed by Miss Vesper countless times. *Remember, my dear, you do not really and truly exist. You are a figment of my imagination, tethered here by the finest thread.*

And she did not know when that thread might unravel or snap.

Only Miss Vesper could make her real. Or rather, Miss Vesper's magic. The very thought of it gave her shivers.

Guy seemed to make little of her admission. "That's the silliest thing I've heard. You are *more* than real."

"What is that supposed to mean?" Her eyes narrowed.

"Only that you are more brave, more strange, and right now, more stubborn than anyone I have ever met," he grumbled.

"Yes. I am quite aware of how strange I am. Thank you very much," she said curtly.

She stepped out from under the moss-covered branches of the dead tree, upset even though she knew he had spoken nothing but the truth. Still, she did not want to talk to him anymore just then. She began to walk down the hill to lose her way among the tombstones. Her stride was awkward, and for once, she did not care.

"Wait." Guy ran after her.

At first she thought he was calling after her to apologize, but when she glanced over her shoulder, the look on his face told her otherwise. His eyes were wide with surprise, not remorse.

"It's on your dress!" His arms waved wildly.

"What?" She reached behind her. Her skin prickled, and something tugged her hair. "What is it? Get it off me!" She fumbled, trying in vain to swat at whatever it was that clung to her dress.

Guy rushed to her side and smacked her hard across the back with the flat of his hand (harder than he had to, she thought). She flinched, not from the contact, although it did hurt rather a lot, but from what he had flung to the ground.

The Hand.

It tumbled to the grass by her feet, stunned by the blow and the fall. However, it soon recovered and began to sidle away. Before it could get very far, Guy bent down and snatched it into the air. He held it with the palm facing up. It wiggled like an overturned bug that could not right itself.

White strands of hair were caught between the fingers.

Irréelle rubbed her head where the hair had been ripped from her scalp.

"It did not sneak away." She scrunched up her face, thinking back to when the scuttling went quiet. And then she remembered something—that she had mistaken for the wind—had brushed against her leg as she climbed up the hollow tree, which was more than likely the Hand first taking hold. She cringed.

"It must have decided to hitch a ride." Guy adjusted his hold on the Hand. It squirmed and twitched, trying to claw him. "Keep still," he said, but it did not listen.

She swept her hands over her dress again even though there was nothing else there to cast away besides dirt. "Why did you lead us to the coffin?" As silly as it seemed to ask these questions of the Hand, she had the distinct feeling it understood each and every word. "Why are you now following us?"

"It must be spying for Miss Vesper." Guy held the Hand in front of him, and it took a swipe at his face. "It'll do whatever she wants it to do. Even lead her to us so she can capture us once again."

The hairs on the back of Irréelle's neck rose, as though Miss Vesper might appear at any moment.

The Hand struggled for release and came much too

close to Guy's face. It pinched his nose. Guy yelped and dropped it fast.

The Hand landed with a thump.

"Quick, quick. Get it back!" Irréelle reached out, but the Hand slipped past, and all she grabbed was a fistful of grass. Guy stomped down, just missing the tips of its fingers with the heel of his boot.

It fled back up the hill, barely visible in the tall grass, and they charged after it. Irréelle's calves ached and Guy's joints creaked. His knees locked up again and he stumbled on the incline. The Hand reached the top of the hill well ahead of them. It circled the dead oak and then scampered up the trunk as natural as a squirrel, crouching low on a thin black branch. With whatever strange senses it had, it observed them.

Guy attempted to snatch the Hand from its perch, but missed. "Come down from there!" The Hand only proceeded to climb higher, digging in with its fingernails and leaving long scratches in the black bark.

Fists on his hips, Guy watched its progress. It stopped halfway up the trunk and then inched out onto a thin branch.

"Maybe we should just leave it be," Irréelle said. "And maybe then it will leave us be."

"And let Miss Vesper find us? No way."

Guy snatched a stone from the ground. He glared up at the Hand, aimed, and chucked the rock straight for it. The rock sailed past, thrown too far left.

"I don't think you should do that," she said, and rounded the oak, keeping her eyes on the Hand as it scurried higher.

"I'll get it down one way or the other." Guy searched for another rock.

She was about to scold him, a tug of guilt, perhaps, for breaking two of the Hand's fingers, when she saw the gravestone. It fell in the shadow of the dead oak, narrow enough that the tree blocked it from view from the other side. But of course there should be a gravestone here. Even though the bones were quite curiously missing from the silk-lined casket, Irréelle and Guy stood directly above a grave after all.

"Come over here," she said.

"Hold on." He took aim again and lobbed a stone at the Hand. Instead of dodging out of the way, it caught the stone and hurled it back at Guy. It grazed his temple. Rubbing his head, Guy came up beside Irréelle. "That thing's got better aim than I do."

His arm dropped to his side when he noticed the

gravestone. It was rather plain, a simple slab of marble the color of slate, but it was perfectly carved. The edges were sharp. Someone had etched each letter of the epitaph precisely.

"Whose bones were stolen, then?" Guy asked.

Irréelle leaned forward to read the inscription in the weather-worn stone. And then she read it again. She lost her breath.

"What? Who is it?" Guy came around and read the engraving. His mouth dropped open.

Irréelle placed a hand to her heart and squeezed shut her eyes. But the name had already burned into her mind.

Arden Mae Vesper

In her head, Irréelle counted to ten, and then she opened her eyes. She took a step closer to the gravestone. There was more to the inscription than the name, and she read each lovely, sorrowful line.

ARDEN MAE VESPER

Night folds close
& with sorrow
holds my hand
empty of yours

Most dearly
& forever more
fair blooms
my love

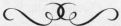

A sprig adorned with leaves and blossoms was etched beneath these words, every line so delicately carved the five-petaled flowers looked real enough to pluck.

The air swirled cold around her ankles. Overhead, the oak's black branches swayed and groaned. Irréelle shook her head and buttoned her lips. She did not want to say it aloud. She did not want it to be true.

But Guy leaned forward and spoke the words Irréelle would not.

"Miss Vesper is dead."

14

Little Monsters

The words sent a jolt down Irréelle's crooked spine. "But she's *not*." Even to her own ears, her protest sounded weak. "Miss Vesper can't be dead," she said more firmly, glaring at the tombstone that so clearly stated otherwise.

Guy looked fascinated instead of horrified. "Maybe you ought to read that line again. 'Holds my hand *empty* of yours.'" Guy tapped his foot on the ground. "Just like the empty casket beneath us."

She felt ill just thinking of it, the coffin's closed lid and the pounds and pounds of dirt that must have been shoveled atop it, trapping Miss Vesper inside. Irréelle gulped, imagining the pinched air and the complete darkness. And the bugs worming their way through the wood. No wonder Miss Vesper never set foot in the underside of the graveyard. It would be like revisiting a nightmare.

Irréelle looked at the sky through the oak's gnarled branches. She pushed away thoughts of tight, cramped spaces. "How can she be dead when I saw her this morning?"

"Well, she must have died. But I guess she's not fully dead." Guy's gray eyes shone in the dark.

"How did she . . . die?" The last word came out as a whisper.

They exchanged a look. "I don't know." Guy's lips twisted to the side as he thought about it. "Maybe she choked on a chicken bone. Maybe she drowned or was murdered in the night."

Irréelle flinched, each of his ideas more dreadful than the one before. "Stop, you're being awful."

Guy grinned, as if he quite enjoyed being awful. "Maybe she was struck by lightning. Maybe she fell out of this very tree and broke her neck." He sucked in a breath, probably ready to rattle off a hundred more tragedies, but Irréelle went still.

"Yes," she said. "Oh my goodness, how horrible."

"She choked on a chicken bone?"

Irréelle's hands went to her throat. "No. I think she

snapped her neck." All this time, the truth had been right in front of her. Miss Vesper had all but told her. "She must be the careless girl who fell down the spiral staircase."

They stood there a moment, letting it sink in.

"Miss Vesper's not a *girl*," Guy said at last. "She's old."

Irréelle looked at the dates on the tombstone. "It happened so very long ago. Perhaps, after all these years, she feels as if she were much younger then." Like Miss Vesper had lived a whole other lifetime, one she had not meant to leave so soon. And now, the bone dust made her ageless.

"Well, I suppose. But how is she walking around the house, dead but not dead?" Guy asked.

Irréelle shivered. "Magic."

For what else could it be? Everything Miss Vesper did was laced with magic: wilting flowers with one touch, turning cinnamon to blood, altering the structure of hair so it grew into skin. She could move the very soil of the earth and make it fly. She must have been filled with magic, enough to rosy dead cheeks and animate a corpse. Enough to imagine Irréelle alive, and when she tired of her, to imagine her away. Or maybe, just maybe, she could imagine her fully real.

And after that, it would be up to Irréelle to design the rest of her life. The possibilities stretched before her, overwhelming and exhilarating. She might try her hand at painting, or ride wobbly on a bicycle; she might learn to swim, diving into the lake and kicking all the way to its sandy bottom. No matter what the adventure, she imagined a boy with a raspy laugh goofing off beside her.

But first, what could Irréelle do to convince Miss Vesper?

"It must have been dark magic, then, bound with bone dust." Guy raised his arms like he was invoking a spell. "Look at all that bone dust can do. It brought Miss Vesper back from the dead. It allowed her to make little monsters."

"What little monsters?" Irréelle looked all around, as if the dirt-made bats might thunder up the hollow of the tree and find her and Guy huddled beside the grave.

He smiled as if he had been hoping she would ask. "Us."

Her limbs went cold. Not because she disagreed, but because she agreed so completely. Perhaps in agreement as well, the Hand scuttled to a lower branch (almost in reach now, but Guy was too busy staring at the gravestone to realize).

Just below the Hand, on the trunk of the tree, Irréelle's eyes fell on a marking she had not previously seen. She stepped closer to get a better look.

Guy continued. "But who used the bone dust to awaken Miss Vesper?"

Irréelle touched the blackened oak. It was difficult to see in the dark, but something had been carved into the wood.

"N.M.H.," she said.

Guy fell silent.

"Look here." She traced her finger over the bark and read aloud. "N.M.H. + A.M.V."

She was used to seeing the initials *N.M.H.* around the house (embossed on the stationery, stenciled on the bone china, embroidered on the hand towels), but she did not expect to see those letters engraved into a tree in the above side of the graveyard. Although, of course, it was not quite as shocking as seeing Miss Vesper's grave when no more than a day ago Irréelle had seen her very much alive . . . or, she now supposed, very much undead.

"A.M.V. is Miss Vesper, of course, but who is N.M.H.?" Guy asked.

The letters were enclosed in an engraved heart. Just like the hearts leading through the tunnel to Miss Vesper's grave. A path made by N.M.H. to retrieve the bones. "Someone who loved her." The inscription on the grave said as much. *Most dearly and forever more fair blooms my love.*

Guy did not look impressed with her response. "Well then, where is he?"

That question she could not answer. But it might hold the key to getting back in Miss Vesper's good graces.

15

The Other Task

Irréelle touched the headstone.

"How sad that Miss Vesper's grave is marked with a dead tree. And that her headstone is all alone atop this hill," she said. "How lonesome." Like an echo of her own life.

From this spot on the hill, she could see all of the cemetery below and each straight row and each crooked headstone, and beyond to the very edge of her neighborhood, where the rooftops and chimneys touched the night sky. The hill was an isolated spot when everything else crowded together. Miss Vesper's grave rested apart from it all.

"What does she care? She's not buried here. It's just

an empty grave." Guy kicked the tree trunk, and the branches shook.

"I don't know. It just matters." She thought of the leafy trees shading the backyard of Miss Vesper's house, in particular the hawthorn with its white blooms, and the flower garden outside the window of the study. "A grave should be marked with daffodils in summer and sprigs of holly in winter."

"And what about spring and autumn?" He smirked.

Irréelle ignored the fact that he thought her silly. "Perhaps foxglove in spring, and I should think chrysanthemums in the fall would be appropriate."

Guy rolled his eyes. "If you say so."

And then, catching Irréelle quite off guard, the Hand slipped down the side of the tree. It jumped to the ground, landed deftly on its fingertips, and ran across the toes of Guy's boots as if to taunt him. It charged off before either of them could move to grab it.

"I'm not done with you yet," Guy said, racing down the hill, away from Miss Vesper's headstone and the empty grave beneath it. Irréelle sprinted after.

As she flew down the slope, she pushed back thoughts of Miss Vesper. For a moment, she was not even thinking of the Hand, only of the wind on her face and the speed of her legs, which propelled her so fast she thought she would lose control. But she did not tame her runaway legs. She gave in to the moment, breaking free of herself.

Her heart pounded, a fierce beat that woke all her nerve endings. *This* was what it meant to be human, to venture beyond the confines of a tiny room in a gloomy house, and to feel and see and breathe in the world.

And then her ankle turned, and the sky and earth swapped places as she fell. Irréelle tumbled down the hill, laughing all the way.

She rolled to a stop, bruised and grass-stained and smiling.

Guy had abandoned his chase for the Hand and stood above Irréelle, grinning and snorting. "Have . . . to . . . be . . . quiet." The words slipped out between chortles of laughter.

Irréelle climbed to her feet, fizzy-headed and bubbling with joy. "The bones don't mind."

"Probably not." Guy's laughter died. "But the night watchman does."

All those bubbles floating inside Irréelle went flat. She cast her eyes through the darkness.

"Let's get out of the open. The last thing we want is for the watchman to find us."

Irréelle slunk after Guy. "What would he do with us?"

Guy looked at her sidelong, eyes glinting the way they always did before he said something terrible. Irréelle squirmed.

Guy raised his hand. "I've heard his touch can turn you to stone. Some of the tombstones, like that one with the weeping girl atop it . . ." He pointed, waiting for Irréelle to turn her head. "She used to be *alive*."

Irréelle scooted away from the statue, as if the watchman might reach around it and place his hand to her skin.

"Don't you know anything about the watchman?" Guy glanced over his shoulder, as if mentioning the watchman might draw him. He grabbed Irréelle's hand and tugged her toward a small wooden arbor dripping with wisteria. They ducked between the vines. "Has Miss Vesper never sent you on the *other* task?"

"I don't even know what the other task is. She said she did not trust me with it." Irréelle pinched the top of her thigh to focus on that insignificant pain instead of the ache in her chest.

"Why wouldn't she trust you?"

Her shoulders slumped. "She does not want others to see me." Not her crooked spine nor her ghost-white hair. And certainly not her misaligned limbs and awful limp.

He met her eyes, muddled though they were. "I was happy to see you."

"You're only saying that because you would have been happy to see *anyone* if they got you out."

"Not anyone." Guy looked at his hands. "I would still be buried in the tunnels if it weren't for you, and I'm grateful. I'd do almost anything to help you."

When he paused, she finished his sentence for him. "Except come back with me."

He frowned regretfully but did not disagree. "Sorry." He ground the heel of his boot into the dirt.

"But why?" His refusal tugged something loose in her chest. A space she had thought only Miss Vesper could fill.

"She left me there," he said simply, a world of hurt in those few words.

Despite the sharpness of her disappointment, she did not want to make him feel worse. "I'm sorry." She placed one hand on his arm.

"It's not your fault," he said. "Only Miss Vesper is to blame for sending us on these tasks in the first place."

His words sparked something inside her, the ember of an idea. "What's the other task? If I complete it, maybe. . . ." But Irréelle could say no more. It was too much to voice—the idea that Miss Vesper might magic her real, that Irréelle would never again have to worry about being imagined away. She could live a normal life, able to exist outside the shadows, no matter what she looked like or who might see her.

She looked at Guy expectantly and lowered her voice. "Don't you feel it?"

"Feel what?"

It knotted in her stomach, the pull of some invisible thread. The tether that connected her to Miss Vesper and allowed her to command Irréelle's bones when they were near. The binding that would never allow Guy to run off, even though he desperately wanted to. "Like there is a string tugging you back."

"No," he said, but she did not believe him.

"We only exist because she allows it."

Guy touched the scrape on his temple. "You think she can snap her fingers and disappear you? That's ridiculous." But she heard the doubt in his voice.

"Please tell me what the other task is." He mumbled something under his breath that referred to Irréelle being *more and more stubborn*. "I heard that," she said, and hid the smile that had started to form behind her hand. While she knew it was a trait Miss Vesper would despise (for she had once told Irréelle, *You have no will of your own, nor any thoughts*

worth thinking), she liked the idea of herself as someone different. Someone separate from Miss Vesper's ties.

"Fine then, but the task is impossible." He released a
great sigh. "You'll need to find the unmarked grave that is
very clearly marked."

16

An Unmarked Grave

Irréelle hoped she had heard him incorrectly. "An unmarked grave that is very clearly marked? But that makes no sense at all." No matter which way she turned it around in her mind, it remained contradictory.

"I know. It makes my head ache just thinking about it. And I had a lot of time to think."

She rubbed her temples. "Did you come up with anything, then? Any ideas?"

"No. Nothing. I've looked everywhere and never found it. Or maybe I have and just didn't realize it. Sometimes I think she sent me out knowing I would fail." Guy continued to dig his heel into the dirt.

Her head snapped up. "I think this task is something

very important to her. Something she entrusted to you."
And not to me, she thought, not without a little envy.

Guy bent down and stuck his fingers into the small hole he had made in the ground. "Her mistake, then."

"Help me find it."

"Got it," he said, but he was not responding to Irréelle. He pulled a worm out of the soil. Pinched between two of his fingers, it squirmed.

"Don't!" she said. Her stomach clenched tight.

He dropped the worm into his open mouth and swallowed. "Want one?"

"That's disgusting. No, thank you." She sat on the bench, turning away from Guy before he gobbled up another worm. Her left foot touched the dirt, her right foot dangled just above it. "Will you help me or won't you?"

Guy stood up. His bones creaked as he walked over to the other bench and sat down. They faced each other. "And what if you find what she wants? What will she need you for then?"

Irréelle had not thought of it, and another worry bloomed alongside all the others, but she did not show it. "She'll still need bone dust, won't she? I'm mostly good at collecting that." Only the idea of spending her days in the underside of the graveyard no longer appealed to her. All she could think about was having a life beyond those dark passages.

She chewed her lip. It would have to be a trade of sorts. If only Irréelle could lead Miss Vesper to the unmarked grave, she would ask Miss Vesper for a magical bone dust blend in return. One that would make her real.

It no longer seemed like a fanciful dream. Almost, almost, she believed it possible.

"Please," she said.

Guy considered. "I'll help you. But after that, I'm leaving."

"Where will you go?" Irréelle felt a pang in her chest.

"No idea." He lay back on the bench, one leg bent, one leg hanging over the side. He draped his arm across his eyes and yawned. "But you should come with me. Don't go back to Miss Vesper."

Irréelle considered for a moment, imagining the adventures she and Guy would have beyond Miss Vesper's house, beyond the graveyard, beyond the only little world they had ever known. She did not want to tell him it was hopeless. One day, Miss Vesper would simply sever the tether and imagine them away. It was precisely the reason they needed to come to an accord.

"Guy? What makes her think there is an unmarked

grave?" she asked instead of answering.

He yawned again. "She said she feels it in her bones."

Irréelle nodded (even though Guy could not see her with his arm over his eyes), as she thought it reasonable that bones could tell such secrets. After all, she too felt their pull in the underside of the graveyard, all the stories and emotions humming through them. "Whose grave is it? Do you know?"

"Don't know." He rolled to his side, turning his back to her. "Now let me rest for a few minutes. Or a few days. My head hurts."

She was surprised he had admitted it, so only said, "Okay." She pressed her lips together to keep from saying more. Although she was tired too, exhausted actually, there was no way she could sleep. She wanted to run into the graveyard and begin the search at once. Of course, she had no idea where to start or what to look for. Why was this unmarked grave so important to Miss Vesper?

Irréelle fidgeted on the bench, not sure how long Guy needed to rest, and not sure what to do to occupy the time. She ran her fingers over the cold stone where someone had long ago engraved a dedication. Moonlight leaked through the wisteria vines and it provided just enough light to see by.

In memory of Aurora Anna Calhoun. No matter where you wander, you reside in my heart.

The letters were worn down by the elements. She traced their edges again, trying to imagine what it would be like to be so well loved. The way N.M.H. must have loved Miss Vesper, enough to defy death. Suddenly, she felt very empty inside.

She stood up, averting her eyes from the bench, and looked through the vines again. Although it was dark, the night did not compare to the absolute blackout of the tunnels without a candle, so she could see quite well in the above side of the graveyard. The moon had risen higher in the sky. It drenched the tombstones with silvery light. There was no sign of the watchman on the path, and there was no sign of the Hand.

Yet she suddenly had the feeling that someone was watching her. (Not Guy, for he was still snoring behind her.) Her skin tingled with gooseflesh. For all she knew, the Hand was tip-fingering closer, crouched low in the grass, hidden in the shadow of a tombstone. Or else the watchman, who must have known every inch of the cemetery, had dimmed his light and sneaked closer, one hand out ready to turn her to stone.

Part of her wanted to retreat to the corner of the arbor and wait for Guy to wake, but another part of her, the part that remembered the feeling she had when Guy called her

brave (and stubborn), did not want to sit still any longer.
She took a bold step through the arch.

Ahead, an owl hooted. Irréelle looked up, up, up.
Atop one of the tallest branches of a nearby tree, the owl
observed the cemetery. It spread its wings and rose into
the air, screeching as it dove. She raised her arms, but it
sought smaller prey. It swooped toward the ground and
then lifted up with powerful wings, something small and
brown in its clutches.

Irréelle thought the little animal was done for, but
somehow it twisted free of the owl's claws and dropped a
very long way to the ground. The owl circled above. Irréelle
ran over to where the animal had fallen. The owl circled
again, and she waved her arms, hoping to scare it off. It
screeched one last time over its lost prey and flew away.

She crouched down and cautiously parted the grass,
afraid the poor animal was dead. Only it was not an animal
at all. Again it was the Hand.

It lay very still. Its bent fingers curled into its palm and
it was streaked red with blood where the owl's talons had
nicked it. For all the trouble it had caused, she could not
leave it there, wounded and alone.

She scooped it into her skirt and dabbed at the cut
with the cleanest part of her hem. Once she wiped the

blood away, the cut was actually quite small. However, she still could not tell how badly it was hurt (or if it was dead, which she did not want to consider), as it lay in her lap unmoving.

And then it gave a little twitch. *Maybe it was only playing dead*, she thought.

"It's okay." She spoke in the same soft tone she used with the skeletons when gathering bone dust. "The owl's gone."

There was no way to know if the Hand understood, but it tucked its fingers together instead of darting away or scratching at her face, which was an improvement over its previous behavior. She slipped the Hand into the pocket of her dress and went to wake Guy. Whether he needed more rest or not, she could not wait any longer.

When she reached the arbor, she pushed back the vines and stepped through the arch. A strangled breath escaped from between her lips.

Guy lay in the same position on the bench, still as could be, turned to stone by the watchman.

17

N.M.H.

Guy's skin was gray, his body unmoving.

Irréelle slipped closer. Her heart pounded in double time to her timid steps. She should not have left him alone while he slept. It was her fault the watchman had found him while he was so vulnerable. It was her fault Guy had turned to stone.

She leaned over him. "Oh, Guy," she whispered, her throat raw with unshed tears.

A great snore shattered the quiet.

Irréelle shrieked and Guy shot upright. "What? What is it? What's wrong?" Wild-eyed, he looked all around, finally focusing on Irréelle.

Her cheeks flushed with heat. "I thought . . . I

thought the watchman had turned you to stone." However, upon closer inspection, she realized his gray skin was more a matter of dirt and moonlight than graveyard granite.

"I'd never let him get close enough."

In relief, a single tear rolled down her cheek. Before she could wipe it away, the Hand darted out of her pocket, crept up her arm, and then, perched on her shoulder, it brushed the tear from her face. She blinked at the Hand.

Guy jumped at the sight of it. "Did that just crawl out of your pocket?" He shifted from foot to foot, hands out, preparing to make a grab for it if it leapt to the ground.

"Yes. It was resting."

He seemed torn about whether to leave it be or to smack it from Irréelle's shoulder. When it made no move to attack or flee, he held his index finger out toward it, much like he would approach a dog to prevent getting bitten, allowing the animal to smell him before scratching it behind the ears or rubbing its belly.

Irréelle sniffed. "Careful, it's hurt. An owl tried to eat it for supper."

Guy's eyes widened. He withdrew his hand and stuffed it into the pocket of his pants. Two of his fingers poked out the hole in the bottom.

"I saved it and now it seems to be playing nice." From

the corner of her eye, she saw the Hand lift its fingers from her shoulder and curl like a claw. Before she could stop it, the Hand reached out. Her head jerked to the side and she grimaced. The Hand combed its fingers through a snarl in Irréelle's white hair. Though it was not overly gentle, she bit her tongue and let it work out the knot to show her own good faith toward bettering the relationship.

Guy watched it skeptically. "Are you sure you can trust it?"

The Hand paused as if offended by the question, so she responded hastily in the affirmative. "Yes, yes, I'm sure." But of course, she was not sure at all.

He raised an eyebrow but said no more about it.

The Hand raked its fingers through another tangle until the strands of hair were more or less smooth. Then it scurried down her arm and tucked itself back into her pocket. She patted it in thanks.

"Well, since I haven't turned to stone," Guy said, smiling while Irréelle rolled her eyes, "we may as well begin our search for the unmarked grave."

"That is very clearly marked," Irréelle added.

They walked over to the archway and peered out at the graveyard through the web of vines. All was quiet. Guy stepped out first, and Irréelle followed. The moon glowed directly overhead in the one cloudless slip of sky. While its soft light allowed them to see quite well, it also made it easier to be seen.

Irréelle looked left and right down the stony path. "Where do you suppose the watchman is?"

"He could be anywhere." Guy turned down the first row of tombstones. "So we'll keep clear of the path. And we'll start in the place I left off."

"What should I be looking for?"

"I don't really know. Anything irregular. Something out of place."

But there was so much ground to cover, too much to explore before sunrise. It would take weeks to properly search the cemetery. Maybe months, if she had no better luck than Guy had. The task felt suddenly overwhelming.

"Isn't it all rather strange?" she asked as they passed an enormous gravestone topped with a single stone crow on one side and a much smaller gravestone wrapped in iron briars on the other.

"I suppose." Guy's eyes were downturned, as if he might stumble across the unmarked grave.

"Why would there be a grave without a headstone?"

"Maybe we're looking for a criminal. Someone dishonorable."

"Miss Vesper would not be trying to find the grave of a criminal."

"Are you so sure?" Guy glanced over his shoulder at Irréelle.

She was no longer sure of anything. They lapsed into silence. She gazed at each headstone they passed, taking note that they were all marked, not that she had expected otherwise.

As they continued to wander through the graveyard, Irréelle tried to imagine she was on the underside, and by doing so she began to orient herself as if she were walking through the tunnels. Up and down the rows they went, until they had reached the far west side, just where she imagined the oldest tunnel to be. To the southeast, beyond the fence that surrounded the entire cemetery, was Miss Vesper's house, snug among its neighbors. To the northeast was the dead oak and Miss Vesper's grave, separate from all the others. And empty.

"Here's where we should start." Guy stopped between two headstones. One was topped with a stone wreath, the other with a statue of a robed figure, head bowed. Irréelle wondered if the figure had once been real, but then shook the thought away.

"One thing first." She chewed on her lip. "What do

you think happened to N.M.H.? If he brought Miss Vesper to life, why is she all alone?"

Gray clouds blotted out the moon. They moved quickly and cast shadows across Guy's face. He swiped one finger across his throat as if it were a knife cutting into skin. "He's probably at the bottom of the unmarked grave."

She gaped at him, horrified he could believe such a thing. "You think Miss Vesper killed him?"

Guy narrowed his eyes. They darkened like a coming storm. "It's exactly the type of thing she would do. She has no heart."

"She wouldn't," Irréelle insisted. She remembered the heart that someone had carved around the initials. "Not if she loved him."

"She doesn't love anyone." Guy's mouth twisted into a frown.

A lump formed in her throat, a reminder of all she was missing. If she did not already know how much Guy despised Miss Vesper and cared nothing for her approval, she might have thought his feelings were hurt.

"She probably can't remember where she buried him and sent us on this goose chase to find his grave and stop him from haunting her."

Irréelle did not want to argue anymore, so she did not

remind him that there were no such things as ghosts.

She turned it around and around in her mind: who N.M.H. might be, if he rested at the bottom of the unmarked grave, whether or not Miss Vesper loved him. And more than anything, she wondered how Miss Vesper had passed through the veil from death to life.

She let these thoughts simmer as she walked along, listening to the bones buried deep in the earth. She was so familiar with them from all her time in the underside of the graveyard that she recognized their unique vibrations, as though some connection existed within her, binding her to the dead. But none of the bones called to her or whispered solemnly. They all seemed quite at peace, resting where they were meant to rest.

She was glad for that, of course, but it also made her uneasy. What if N.M.H. was not buried here at all?

Irréelle clenched her fists, refusing to consider that possibility. She rounded on the closest headstone, scouring it with her eyes as if the bones might reach through dirt and scratch a map to the unmarked grave on its surface.

But of course, all she saw were the weather-worn letters carved long ago, set in remembrance of a *kind soul, gone too soon*. The epitaph could have been written for almost anyone, too vague to be of any help.

Irréelle scanned the gravestone beside it with equal intent. And then all the rest in the row. Some inscriptions were plain but heartfelt. Others praised the good deeds of the deceased or the manner of their fine work, such as *the soft-hearted baker* and *the nimble-fingered locksmith*.

And though it was almost like reacquainting with old friends, the more headstones she surveyed, the more hopeless her task seemed. Guy appeared to be faring no better, grumbling as he marched along.

She let out a shaky sigh but pushed on to the next one. With the clouds darkening the sky and the crumbling of the old gravestone, Irréelle had to lean very close to read the inscription. It was simple and sweet in its brevity, and she did not think much of the words until she read the one beside it, etched in the same slanted script.

Beneath her feet the bones hummed in perfect synchrony.

Irréelle's heart galloped in her chest. "Guy," she whisper-hissed, wanting his attention, but ever mindful of the watchman, wherever he roamed. Guy turned away from the stone he had been inspecting and jogged over to her side.

"Look here." She waved her arm toward the graves. The markers were so closely spaced that the stones almost kissed.

"We're looking for one grave, not two," Guy said, as if she needed a reminder.

Before he could shrug away her excitement, she dragged him closer. Maybe he would feel the interwoven pulse of the underground bones.

He looked from one marker to the other and then his eyebrows shot up in understanding. "Lovebirds?"

"Yes," Irréelle said. "Maybe in just this way, N.M.H. buried himself by Miss Vesper."

They grinned at each other and then at the gravestones.

Beside the crooked marker for *a most devoted husband* leaned its mirror image for his *most beloved wife*. Whether married or otherwise, those in love lay side by side, unwilling to let death keep them apart.

N.M.H. would not be tucked away in the cemetery, a stranger among the bones. He would rest by Miss Vesper (or at least, by her plot beneath the oak) without thought or worry that he might remain forever nameless in an unmarked grave.

For all the love Miss Vesper had denied her, Irréelle still warmed inside that someone could care so much for another. Something far beyond words.

Like friendship, Irréelle realized. She did not need Guy to declare they were friends. It was enough that he stood beside her. The knowing, the *feeling* of friendship and love mattered most of all.

"Come on," Guy said, tearing away.

They were halfway down the row, running back toward the hill, when Irréelle stiffened. The tiny white hairs on her arms stood up. "Do you feel that?"

"What?" Guy's mouth formed the word, but a clap of thunder drowned out his voice.

The air vibrated with its shuddering boom. Guy stumbled. Irréelle covered her ears. Only it was not the thunder that had startled her but the slap of wings on air. She tipped her face to the sky.

A cloud of bats circled above them.

18

The Girl with Dark, Dark Eyes

Irréelle stared up at the dirt-made bats, which hardly looked like bats at all. They loomed above, somehow even more misshapen, as if they had smooshed themselves together when fighting their way from the underside of the graveyard. They each had four wings instead of two. And two hideous heads instead of one. They glared at Irréelle with hollow eyes.

"Miss Vesper's creatures," she said. Dread coiled in her stomach.

The bats dove, mouths likes gashes as they poured from the sky. Irréelle stumbled backward. Guy held his ground, grabbing a rock from the grass and heaving it at the bats. It sailed right past.

"Come on." Irréelle tugged his arm. He tossed one more stone, for all the good it did, and then they ran.

Legs pounding, they twisted back and forth between the gravestones. But with nothing to impede their progress, the bats drew closer and closer until they were upon Irréelle and Guy. Their double wings grazed her hair. She swatted and slapped, but the bats dodged her fists. They dug their claws into the sleeves of her dress, and next to her, they reached for Guy.

Her feet lifted an inch off the ground and then another. She squirmed, punching at their earthen bodies. Dirt broke off in chunks, but the bats held on.

Guy kicked his legs and thrashed all about. He made such a fuss, and his shirt was so threadbare, the bats lost their grip, and he tumbled to the ground.

"Irréelle!" he called as the bats dragged her along. He snatched up pebbles from the walkway and chucked them overhanded, but the stones bounced off Irréelle's shins and her boots rather than striking the bats. She winced as a rock glanced off her knee.

Guy scowled. He took aim again, and Irréelle shut her eyes, tensing, but this time the stone thudded into dirt. She opened her eyes in time to see a bat spiral to the ground.

And then another and another crashed through the air, splattering on the gravestones.

Only, Guy's hands hung by his sides. His head swiveled as a flurry of stones arced over their heads. They struck the bats right between the eyes, and the creatures lost their hold on Irréelle.

She landed in a heap, careful not to smash the Hand in her pocket. Dirt dropped onto her shoulders as more stones met their mark. The bats broke apart, their bodies crumbling. Guy ran to her side and pulled her to her feet.

A bolt of lightning split the sky in two. It illuminated the gleaming gravestones and a girl standing among them. With one arm tucked tight to her side and the other raised for battle, she looked like a mighty soldier facing a vast army. Her arm shot out, knocking another bat from the sky, and then she turned toward them, staring straight at Irréelle with dark, dark eyes.

"Are you going to help me or do I have to do it all myself?" the girl asked, a grin wide on her face.

Irréelle and Guy ran to her side and grabbed a few stones piled by the girl's feet. Standing all in a row, they faced off against the bats as it began to rain. It soaked them in seconds.

Irréelle hurled a pebble, nicking the wings of a

charging bat. Guy threw stone after stone, each one flying more wild than the one before. And the girl who had come from nowhere raised her whip-fast arm over and over, never missing her target.

Guy clenched his jaw and side-eyed the girl. "Who are you?"

The girl's tongue poked out of her mouth as she aimed. "I'm Lass." Another bat plummeted to the grass.

The ones that remained circled warily and clumsily. They flew for shelter, but too late. Bit by bit the wind and rain washed them from the sky. They slopped to the ground, dirt turned to mud. Their remains clotted the grass.

The water running down Irréelle's face could not diminish her smile. "Thank you."

Exactly matched to her dark, dark eyes, the girl's short, curly hair was as black as the raven's feather under Irréelle's bed. It glistened in the rain. She wore a long navy coat that fell to her knees with sleeves hanging well past her fingertips. Skinny legs stuck out from the bottom of her coat, and a pair of boots, much like Irréelle's own (except without all the scuff marks), were laced up her ankles.

"You sure needed the help."

Rain dripped off the end of Guy's nose. He glowered. "Did not."

Lass was cleaner than Irréelle and much, much cleaner than Guy. Although she was just as wet, there was hardly a speck of dirt on her coat or face. She did not look like a girl who would visit a cemetery in the middle of the night. Irréelle could not say the same for herself, or for Guy, who looked more like the undead, crawled out of their graves.

"Oh, I should have let those sky-rodents devour you!" the girl said.

"As if they could have." Guy puffed up his chest.

"As if they *would* have." The girl looked Guy up and down. "You don't have any meat on those skinny bones."

Irréelle smoothed her wet hair as best she could, folded her arms across her stomach (the left beneath the right), and wedged herself into the conversation before they said anything worse. "I'm Irréelle, and this is Guy."

The girl nodded, tilting her face to the sky and letting rain splash her cheeks. "Are you the two who've gone missing? You don't appear to be missing, since I've just found you. Or are you someone else?"

"Slow down," Guy said, still snippy. "What are you talking about? What are you doing here?"

Irréelle elbowed him. She did not know why he was acting so rude. Unless he was upset he could not throw as true as the girl.

Lass ignored Guy and spoke directly to Irréelle. "She said you were gone for good."

Irréelle glanced at the girl's boots again, identical to her own, and wondered at their similarity. But Irréelle also noticed the subtle things about the girl, the smallest imbalance in her posture, bones that cracked when she moved, and a trace scent of cinnamon rising from her skin. "You know Miss Vesper."

"That's right." The girl gave another satisfied nod. "So it *is* you."

"Miss Vesper sent you after us?" Hands on his hips, Guy placed himself between Irréelle and the girl. His boots slid on the slick grass.

Irréelle pushed past him.

Lass shook her head. "No, she sent me—"

"After the unmarked grave," Irréelle finished for her. Everything felt more and more curious.

You are not the first; nor will you be the last, Miss Vesper had told her, so very recently. And who could this girl be but someone intended as a replacement for Irréelle, just as Irréelle replaced Guy (duly noted, never to Miss Vesper's satisfaction)? Though the girl looked nothing like her, Irréelle knew inside they were made of the same dust and bone.

"Yes, that's right."

"We're going to find it first," Guy said.

Lass folded her arms, and the long sleeves of her coat flopped to the side. "I doubt that very much."

"You interrupted us."

"I *saved* you," Lass reminded him.

Guy opened his mouth, but before he could snarl out a reply, Irréelle jumped in. "We should work together, shouldn't we?"

"Of course we should," Lass said at once. A smile blazed across her face.

Guy spoke out of the side of his mouth. "How do we know she isn't spying for Miss Vesper?"

"Be nice," Irréelle said.

"Funny how she arrives just as the bats attack us," Guy muttered.

"I can hear you." A dark look crossed Lass's face. "And I'm *not* going to tell Miss Vesper about you."

"Why wouldn't you?" Guy asked. "You're already performing her tasks like a good little puppet."

"That's only because I *have to*." Lass frowned. "Like there's a thread inside my belly, connecting me to her." Irréelle trembled. "But my bones don't trust Miss Vesper, so I don't trust Miss Vesper. Not from my first breath."

"Well, you shouldn't," Guy said. "And you shouldn't return to her. Get as far away from her as you can."

Thunder shuddered in the distance. The storm moved away from them, but the way Guy and Lass argued, Irréelle felt like she stood in the middle of it.

"I can't. She made me a promise—"

"What sort?"

Lass fidgeted. "To give back something I've lost."

"You don't think she'll actually keep the promise, do you?"

Irréelle was so unused to the chatter she could barely keep up with them, but she jumped in before they lost their focus entirely. She blinked raindrops from her lashes. "We need to show you something."

"Show me what?"

"The truth about Miss Vesper."

19

Reunions and Resurrections

Irréelle led them around the dead oak, showing Lass the initials encircled in the heart first. Then they solemnly turned to Miss Vesper's headstone. Raindrops slid down its gray surface, as if it wept.

"Goodness," Lass said. "You think whoever N.M.H. is raised her from the grave?"

"Yes," Irréelle said.

"But who is it?"

"That's what we need to find out."

"Oh my." Lass looked from the headstone to the engraving and back again. "She wants to be reunited with him."

Of course, Lass must be right. A love unbroken by death. *Most dearly and forever more.* "How tragic," Irréelle said.

"More like creepy." Lass crinkled her nose.

Guy stood off to the side, under a thick branch that partially blocked the rain. "Can't you see what she really must want to do?"

"I just told you what she means to do," Lass said. But perhaps she was as curious as Irréelle, for she said (rather huffily), "What do *you* think she wants?"

Guy paused, and Irréelle had the impression he enjoyed drawing it out. He squeezed water from the end of his shirt. "Isn't it obvious?" He offered them a crooked smile. "She wants to resurrect him."

Irréelle shivered. She had watched Miss Vesper bring the Hand to life. Irréelle and Guy and Lass existed only because of the bone dust and Miss Vesper's imaginings. Maybe she could bring back her true love too. If only she knew where he lay buried.

"Then we should help her do so," Irréelle said.

"What?" Guy's head snapped up. "No way."

"Why?" Lass asked at the same time. "Bad idea."

They side-eyed each other, as if they did not trust this moment of agreement between them.

Irréelle rushed on. "I don't mean we should call him from the grave. But—"

Thunder rattled around them and then Guy lowered

his raspy voice. "Maybe we already woke him when we started snooping around. Maybe he's slowly, slowly rising."

Irréelle's eyes flicked over her shoulder as if N.M.H.'s hand might be pushing up from the softened earth.

"Right now, he's tugging his soul away from his bones."

A line of white lightning zigzagged across the sky. Irréelle ducked her head so Guy would not see her mouth pinch tight.

"He's slipping through the night, untouched by the rain. He's coming to find us." Guy drew out each word.

"Well, good," Lass said, without so much as a tremor in her voice. "Then he can lead us right back to his coffin and we'll know exactly where the unmarked grave is located."

"Oh, you're spoiling my fun," Guy said, but for the first time, he grinned at Lass.

However, the grin quickly drooped on his face when Lass whacked his arm with the sleeve of her oversized coat. She looked at Irréelle. "That's what you think we should do, right?"

Irréelle wanted to be as carefree as Guy and as brave as Lass, but right then she settled for being hopeful. "Just think, if we find where he's buried, we can ask her for whatever we like." She pressed her hands together. "And she will have to give it to us. A trade of sorts."

Guy longed for freedom and Lass wanted Miss Vesper to fulfill some sort of promise to return something she had lost, so Irréelle would do all she could to help them. And she would help herself as well. Once, Irréelle may have hoped for Miss Vesper's love, but it could not be bartered or traded. She would ask for magic, enough of it to make her fully real. Maybe then she would be worthy of love. Her heart beating at a pace all its own.

Guy laughed. "You want us to trick her."

"That's not what I meant," Irréelle said, but Guy was not listening, and she supposed he was right in a way.

"It's perfect," Lass said. "The hunt for the grave is on."

"If only we had Miss Vesper's notebook. It might contain some clue." Irréelle did not know what secrets or ideas Miss Vesper might have scratched onto its pages.

"I will get it," Lass said.

"But she always has it with her," Guy pointed out. "You won't be able to."

"Oh yes I will." Lass said it as if she had accepted a challenge.

Lass sounded so absolutely confident, but Irréelle had known Miss Vesper much longer, how watchful she was, how vengeful. "You must be careful."

"No, I must be daring," Lass said. "And very, very sneaky." She smiled, and Irréelle could not help but return it.

Clouds rolled across the sky, chasing the storm and revealing the moon. Pale light sprinkled the cemetery instead of rain. The night had been washed clean and it shimmered with possibility.

Irréelle thought of the hearts in the tunnel and the one marking the tree. They had to mean something. "We think he's resting close to her grave."

Guy lifted a blackened stick from the ground, broken off in the storm. He poked the muddy ground around the tombstone. "He might be right beneath our feet."

"Or maybe near the base of the hill." At the very least, they knew he was not *directly* beside Miss Vesper's headstone, for the grave lay empty.

"Yeah," Guy said. "That's what I meant."

Irréelle and Guy slipped and slid their way down the slope. Lass seemed to have no trouble at all and reached the bottom first.

She lifted the hood on her coat, which was as dark as midnight shadows. "I'll scout ahead."

As fast as Irréelle could blink, Lass disappeared into the maze of tombstones. Irréelle would never be able to blend in so easily. She tugged on a strand of her hair, still very bright despite the mud laced within the strands.

And then she flicked it over her shoulder, following Guy. They were so close to finding the unmarked grave.

It was strange to think that locating these long-dead bones might be the very thing that would convince Miss Vesper to give Irréelle life.

Guy stopped midstride. "Do you hear that?"

Irréelle tilted her head, listening. In her pocket, the Hand twitched, awoken from its slumbering.

Something creaked in the night. Irréelle thought of caskets opening and crypt doors gasping, but nothing moved in the graveyard except branches swaying in the wind. Still, something was out there.

It came on the breeze, a whistle that tinkled like a music box winding down. Only it did not wind down but repeated the same eight notes again and again, a lullaby that would bring nightmares instead of pleasant dreams.

Guy stole behind the closest grave marker and pulled Irréelle beside him. They peeked over the very top of it. A beam of light slid between the headstones. It did not reach the one they hid behind, but they ducked anyway.

"The watchman," Irréelle said. They had practically stumbled across his path. He must have seen the bats across the cemetery and come to investigate once the rain stopped. "We have to find Lass."

They huddled side by side. The light swept to the left of the headstone, and Guy edged back so he was behind Irréelle. The whistling sounded no closer, but neither did it retreat.

And then silence fell.

Irréelle strained to listen. A footstep, a sniffle, even the nightmare-inducing whistle would help to pinpoint where the watchman stood. She rose up and peeped over the top of the headstone.

"Who's there?" The voice came out of the darkness. The watchman had extinguished his light. "Who's there? Who's there, with the ghost-white hair?" he said, sounding eager and giddy, as if they were playing hide-and-seek. He began to whistle again.

She hunched down, heart beating wild (like a burning coal spitting sparks), unsure what they should do next. "Guy?" she whispered. He did not respond.

Irréelle glanced over her shoulder. He was no longer there. Down the row behind her, she saw movement. Without once looking back, Guy streaked between the gravestones.

He had abandoned her.

20

The Watchman

A small breath escaped between her lips.

It could not have been any louder than the rustling of leaves blowing in a breeze or a bird's wing striking the air, but the watchman spoke just after, as if he had heard her. "Who's there? Come out, come out."

The Hand darted from her pocket and up the front of her dress. Then it jumped, not down to the ground but straight for her face. It covered her mouth, fingers spread chin to cheek. She looked at it cross-eyed and latched on to it with both of her hands. She pried and pulled, but it refused to budge.

The watchman's voice came closer, each syllable drawn out. "I'll find you." There was a note of certainty—

and horrid delight—in his tone.

"Find you I will," he sang.

The Hand pressed down against her mouth, but she was glad for it now that she knew it only wanted her quiet. Without it, she might have shouted a warning for Lass or called out for Guy, which would not have helped any of them in the least.

Although she did not understand why he had abandoned her, she tried to believe he had good reason. *So long as he gets away*, she thought, determined to cast off disappointment, *far away, just as he wished it.*

Only she could not let the watchman catch her either. She still had to find the unmarked grave. And besides, what would the watchman think if he saw her up close? He might think she belonged here, an odd assortment of bones come to life, trying to flee from the cemetery.

She stood very still and willed her legs not to tremble. Like a statue, she would become motionless and mute, a girl of stone.

Except she really might turn to stone if the watchman found her.

Her nerves crackled, her pulse raced. Every particle tingled, pins and needles and waiting.

He could be anywhere.

Finger by finger, the Hand released its hold on her mouth. She reached for it and tried to shove it back into the pocket of her dress, but it squirmed out of her grip and attached itself to her shoulder. Irréelle tensed.

The whistling resumed, closer still. Each note rang sharp and clear in the cool night air. Above, the stars twinkled as if dancing to the watchman's tune.

She held her breath. She clenched her fists. She prepared to run.

And then, farther off, she heard footsteps falling fast. The whistling cut off midnote.

Her head snapped to the right, eyes wide. She crouched beside the edge of the tombstone and poked her head out to glimpse the rest of the graveyard. On her shoulder, the Hand leaned forward.

The watchman was there. No more than twenty paces away. He would find her, catch her, scold her bones for escaping under his watch, and then turn her to stone. His head swiveled.

And then he ran, only he took off in the opposite direction from where Irréelle hid. She breathed out.

Her relief lasted only seconds when she realized he ran toward Guy.

Ahead on the stone path, Guy sprinted away. He did

not seek the shadows or stride silently. Instead, he drew the watchman after him.

She cried out, wanting (and not) to recapture the watchman's interest, but the Hand leapt for her face, clamping down on her mouth once again, and smothered the sound. Only when she pressed her lips together, a silent promise that she would not call out again, did the Hand release its hold.

Irréelle crept out from behind the tombstone and followed the watchman, who followed Guy. She kept low and to the shadows, staying among the tombstones instead of returning to the path. She had to stop the watchman.

In a nearby tree, an owl screeched, and in her pocket, the Hand flinched.

"Keep calm," she whispered. The advice was as much for the Hand as it was for herself.

She hurried onward, careful not to step on the gravesites as she wound through the stones. The Hand thumped against her thigh as she ran.

Guy and the watchman flashed in and out of sight. Guy chanced a look over his shoulder, and with a sharp turn, he veered off the path. The watchman did not follow. Instead, he slowed and then continued on the path.

Irréelle came to a halt. She did not know which one to

track. Both of them were edging farther and farther away. She made a split-second decision and tore after Guy.

Although she was unfamiliar with the above side of the graveyard, she thought Guy might be heading back toward the arbor. Maybe he thought it would still be safe. Maybe Lass would find them there.

Knowing the watchman was out there, but not where he was, made her uneasy. She could no longer see him. Wherever he was, he made no sound as he hunted them.

When at last Guy slowed, they were not near the arbor after all. She did not see anywhere to hide unless he intended to climb the tree standing just in front of him.

Unexpectedly, Guy took a step back. The watchman leaned out from behind the tree, having circled around to approach from the rear. Despite the distance, Irréelle could see the smear of his dark smile.

"There you are," the watchman said. He lunged forward and clasped hold of Guy's arm.

Irréelle started forward. "Guy!"

Guy and the watchman lifted their faces to her at the same time. "No," Guy shouted as best he could with his disused voice. "Run!" Irréelle did not want to listen, but he yelled again. "Run!"

She turned on her heel and fled, but not before she

saw Guy slump to the ground. Every step she took away from him, she regretted.

Had he turned to stone already?

Irréelle forced her feet faster. She had to find Lass and warn her. Maybe together they could save Guy. She refused to believe it was too late.

She could not let the watchman catch her too.

If only her hair were not so very white. As she ran, it trailed behind her like the tail of a shooting star. Against the night, there was no hiding it, even in the shadows.

Irréelle fled deeper into the cemetery, in the direction Lass had gone, dodging this way and that, so that if the watchman followed, he could not guess which way she turned. Although he knew every inch of the cemetery, she knew the paths in the underside of the graveyard. She tried to orient herself again, but she was moving so quickly and darting here to there without foresight, and she felt hopelessly lost.

She risked another glance behind her. No sign of the watchman. All she saw were the headstones jutting toward the dark sky.

The impressions of her footsteps pressed into the wet grass. It hit her then, a sinking feeling in her gut, that it did not matter how far she ran or where she chose to hide;

all he had to do was follow the trail she had left him like scattered bread crumbs.

She slipped behind the nearest tombstone. In her pocket, the Hand was squashed between her bent legs and her chest.

Breathe in, breathe out, she reminded herself. There was still a chance he would pass her by. She rounded her shoulders, making herself as small as possible, pressing her back against the stone and into the deepest shadows, as if she could somehow will herself invisible.

The guard did not whistle. He did not call out either.

But he approached.

21

Sneaking and Snooping

A shadow lengthened across the grass. The watchman's shadow.

It stretched and stretched, slanting and distorting its shape across the tombstones so it appeared inhuman, all sharp angles and defined edges. It absorbed the darkness from the night, the very blackest part of it, and shunned the moon above. It spilled like ink around her and spread.

The shadow lingered, so near to her. It stilled. It remained in that one place so long she tried to convince herself she had only imagined it shifting closer. She stared at its edges. Maybe it was only the shadow of a tree. Maybe the branches had been blowing in the wind.

Except there were no trees nearby.

Irréelle lifted her chin from her knees and glanced upward. The watchman's leering face loomed over the top of the tombstone. He tilted his head. "I've got you, I have." One long arm reached out, and with fingers bony and cold, he snatched hold of her wrist before she could scramble away. His fist curled tight and he yanked her to her feet.

"Let go," she whispered, too choked up to gain any volume.

Her skin chilled. She imagined herself turning to stone from the inside out. Her toes numbed in her boots, ice racing up her legs. She would freeze in place, forever after staring down at the lonesome grave beside her.

She pulled and struggled, and only when she tried to pry his fingers from her wrist did she realize he wore gloves, all the better for digging graves. The chill racing through her bones was not the watchman's magic, but rather the breeze blowing across her soaking dress and hair. But there was only one slip of material between their skin.

The watchman stood still and calm, unaffected by her efforts. He might remove his gloves at any moment and turn her to stone at his whim.

"Yes, yes, I've got you." He looked down at her with dull eyes. "But what have I got?" He shuddered, as if he had caught a monster rather than a girl. His fingers loosened, but before she could pull away, they tightened once again. "Hold still, you little nightmare."

Irréelle cringed under his inspection. His lip curled, the way it might after tasting something most displeasing.

Up close in the dark, his skin looked gray, his teeth a shade darker. His face was plain and flat, a smudge of unmemorable features. The kind of face made for the shadows.

"You're quite frightful," he said. "I thought the boy was an oddling, but you look very much like an upright corpse."

Irréelle winced.

"What am I to do with the strange likes of you?" His eye twitched.

"Let me go, and my friend too. We weren't harming anything."

"Ah, but you were trespassing, weren't you? Sneaking and snooping and up to no good. You should have expected there would be a punishment," he said.

Miss Vesper had taught her that well enough. Irréelle only hoped he would be more forgiving and far less creative. She still felt faint at the thought of her bones burning.

The watchman dragged Irréelle through the cemetery

and down a long gravel road that led to the front gate. In places, the metal was speckled red with rust. It looked as if it, and the entire fence, had been standing there forever without repair. The gate leaned outward and Irréelle could not help but think that someone—or *something*—had pushed very hard against it trying to escape.

Just to the side of the gate stood a small, run-down caretaker's cottage, as gray as the watchman himself. Broken shingles spotted the roof. Paint peeled from the rotted siding. The brick chimney sloped to the side. From his pocket, the watchman drew a ring of keys (some of which were toothy and tarnished and looked ancient enough to open the old crypts). He found the appropriate one, but he did not take Irréelle inside.

At the back of the cottage stood a shed. It was built of wood, warped and stained, and overlaid with mismatched planks and rusted nails. He led her to the door, pulling her along when she dug her heels into the ground.

"Stop your squirming." He inserted the key into the lock.

All at once, a body rushed forward, trying to squeeze past the watchman and get outside. Irréelle's heart leapt. It was Guy.

But the watchman was too quick, and without letting

go of Irréelle he placed one hand on Guy's chest and shoved him backward into the shed. "Feisty, feisty. Now, stay put."

He pushed Irréelle ahead and then stepped in beside them. She was relieved to see that Lass was not there.

The space, lit with one dim lamp, was much too small for all three of them, as it was lined with shelves and shovels and rakes, and stacked with headstones yet unmarked and a single wheelbarrow half filled with dirt. There was such a low ceiling, the watchman's head nearly touched the beams above.

His threatening form towered over them.

He shut the door, the wide night sky abandoned on the other side. The one window was so smudged with grime, Irréelle could not catch even a glimpse of the moon.

She backed into a corner. Her feet tangled among the shovels leaning against the wall, but their tips were stabbed right into the earth floor and kept them in place. She, on the other hand, fell to the ground.

Guy glared at the watchman. With his too-short pants and his too-short sleeves, along with his skinny arms and legs, and filthy hair hanging forward in his eyes, Irréelle thought he looked more like a hungry gutter rat than a fierce boy who would stand up to the watchman. But he did it anyway, and she found herself mirroring his expression as best she could as she climbed to her feet.

"Such strange little troublemakers," the watchman said. "What were you up to? What were you looking for?"

"Nothing." Irréelle tried to hold her voice and her gaze steady.

"I'm sure and certain it was *something*," the watchman said. "But what?" When neither of them responded, he continued, "I despise secrets. So tell me, you will." He cocked his head. "Either that, or here you will rot."

Irréelle shuddered.

"You can't keep us here." Guy folded his arms. "You better let us out. We didn't do anything wrong."

The watchman's body blocked the door and he made no move to let them pass, but he said, "And let you out I shall. Eventually. You don't imagine I intend to keep you here once the rot sets in? The smell would be ghastly."

Irréelle's fingers curled around the handle of the closest shovel.

The watchman looked from one of them to the other. "What would I do with the likes of you two? After all, I mind the dead, not the living." His head swung back to Irréelle. "Although I do wonder exactly what you are."

A little monster, Irréelle thought.

"You're not a dead ghostly girl, are you?" Keeping his distance, he inspected every odd angle of her, as if that was exactly what he thought she might be.

She did not want to see herself through his eyes. It mirrored too closely all the things Miss Vesper said about her and made her long for home, where she could bar the door and never have anyone recoil at the sight of her.

"Leave her alone," Guy said.

A low chuckle rumbled in the watchman's throat. "Tired of my hospitality already? Very well." A blurred smile crossed his face. "Only tell me who I need to call to retrieve you. Unless . . ." He paused. "Unless you do belong to the graveyard after all."

Guy shut his mouth tight like it was stuck with glue. Irréelle glanced at him sidelong. She could practically feel him willing her silent. Even the Hand squirmed by the smallest degree in her pocket. She bit her lip, determined not to speak. They had not even found the unmarked grave yet, interrupted by the watchman just when they had narrowed in on its location.

"Come, now," the watchman said. His hand snaked out, adjusting the different items on the shelf by the door. He selected a pair of gardening shears. They clicked open and shut, sharp enough to cut through bone. Rust crisped off from the blades. "Don't make me pry it out of you."

Still Guy said nothing, though his eyes latched on to the tool in the watchman's hand. Irréelle's throat went dry.

Leaning forward, his shears clicking open and closed, open and closed, open and closed, the watchman cocked his eyebrow. "Or is there no one at all who knows you are here?"

Guy edged away from the point of the shears, stumbled against the wheelbarrow, and fell backward into it atop the pile of dirt. His legs dangled over the side.

The watchman moved no closer, but his shadow seemed to slide nearer to Guy. "Is there no one at all who cares what becomes of you?"

"Of course there is," Irréelle lied, but she had never wished more for it to be the truth.

"And who would that be?" The watchman asked in such a way that made it clear he did not believe her. He touched the blade to his own cheek, pressing into the skin, not quite cutting into it, but leaving a long red line from the pressure. "Sharp blades always loosen hesitant tongues."

Irréelle could taste rusted metal in her mouth. Guy shook his head, but the words were already tumbling from between her lips. "Miss Arden Vesper."

"Ah." The watchman twirled the shears around his

finger. "I know that name." He tapped the tool to his lips. "How do I know that name? Let me think, let me think." His hand froze. "Ah, yes."

Irréelle tensed, afraid of what he might say at the same time she hung by a thread waiting for what he might reveal.

"Miss Vesper died a tragic death, did she not?"

"No," Irréelle said. "She is very much alive."

"Nonsense," said the watchman. "It is all coming back to me. I remember her funeral, for I've never missed a farewell in all my many years here. There was a strange sort of gentleman who stood well apart from all the other mourners, as if he alone shouldered the grief. And when they left, he stood there still. It was only later I found what he'd done to the oak, marking it as if the lovely stone I'd carved for her grave was not enough."

The watchman frowned. "It's why I remember her name. That fellow should not have vandalized my tree. Just as you should not have trespassed in my cemetery."

"Did you hurt him?" Irréelle could not stop herself from asking.

"Mind your mouth." The watchman slashed the shears through the air, and Irréelle reeled backward. She clamped her lips together so he could not snip off her tongue.

"But no. No, I couldn't say what became of the man. He

never returned to the cemetery again. Neither when he was alive . . ." The watchman smiled. "Nor when he was dead."

22

Punishment

Irréelle's breath caught. The watchman's words ran through her head. She looked toward Guy, still sprawled in the wheelbarrow. He stared back at her as if the same thought had occurred to him too.

If what the watchman said was true, then they might endlessly search the cemetery and never find N.M.H. He was not buried in the graveyard. All these years, Miss Vesper had sent her *little monsters* searching in entirely the wrong place. Maybe he rested much, much closer to home, for where else could he be if not here?

"How curious it is that you claim to live with Miss Vesper when she's been dead these many years. That you would lie to me, snatching a name from a tombstone without respect for the dead." The watchman seethed. "I must think on a punishment worthy of your misdeeds."

He jangled the ring of keys, tempting them. "Dream all you want of escape, but without a skeleton key you will find no way out."

Then, like fog shifting, he slipped out of the shed and into the night.

"Wait!" Guy cried.

He shot up from the wheelbarrow, overturning it on his way to the door, which closed in his face. From the other side, the lock clicked into place. He pounded once against the wood and then stalked away. His eyes swept past Irréelle without looking at her.

"Please don't be upset that I gave him Miss Vesper's name. He did not even believe me." Irréelle had exposed their connection to Miss Vesper, endangering them both, but the watchman thought her admission a lie. "Just think of the information we gained." She whispered in case the watchman was listening. "We still might be searching for N.M.H. in the cemetery. And he isn't here."

"What good does it do us if we're stuck in here?"

"We'll find a way out." She looked around the shed as if there might be another door that she had somehow overlooked, one that did not require a skeleton key to open.

"I've been all over this place. There's no other way out."

Guy went to the window and wiped at the dirt and dust with his sleeve, but even if they broke the pane of glass, she could see it was much too small to pass through. He simply seemed to want to avoid looking at her. "I thought I could distract him and you would find Lass and hide. I didn't think he'd catch any of us."

"I know," she said, though her cheeks warmed. She had *not* known, not at first. She had not put enough trust in him. "It was a good plan. I spoiled it."

"I thought I was faster than him. He never came close to catching me before."

Irréelle did not want to remind him of the many months he had spent in the underside of the graveyard, immobile. His legs were probably not as strong or sure in their footing. "You were faster. Much faster. He only tricked you by circling around from another direction."

Without warning, the lock rattled on the door. Irréelle jumped.

She stared at the handle, bracing for the watchman's return. It jiggled and clattered for several long minutes, but it did not turn and eventually quieted again. A few moments later, a soft tapping came at the little window. Irréelle's head whipped to the side.

193

Lass's face bobbed into sight on the other side of the glass. Irréelle and Guy rushed over, crowding close together.

"Hurry. Get us out of here," Guy said.

Lass's mouth moved, but she must have been whispering, wary of the watchman. Irréelle could not hear her, but she read her lips. "She can't open the door."

Guy's shoulders slumped.

"It's okay," Irréelle said. "We'll be okay."

If anything, Lass looked even more defeated than Guy. "I'm sorry," she mouthed, and hung her head.

Irréelle touched the window. "Go back to the house so you don't get in trouble with Miss Vesper. She still trusts you."

Lass stood there stubbornly.

"Go, before the watchman sees you," Guy said.

She hesitated another moment and then darted away from the shed.

Irréelle was staring at the spot Lass had so recently occupied when Guy suddenly hurried to the shelf. He began examining the assortment of tools, picking up this and that. "Maybe Lass couldn't bust the lock. Maybe I couldn't push past the watchman, but the two of us together should be able to get by him. We'll just have to better prepare ourselves."

With that, he spun around. A pair of goggles, perhaps used for protection when cutting inscriptions into stone, were propped on his head. In one hand, he held the trowel, and in the other, a spade, which he tossed to Irréelle without warning.

Surprisingly, she caught it.

Geared up, Guy (with his goggles, a trowel, and a rake) and Irréelle (with the spade and a shovel finally wrenched free) stationed themselves in front of the door. They listened for the watchman's tread on the ground and for the clinking of his skeleton keys.

And they waited and waited and waited. Prepared for battle.

When the watchman returned, they had no warning. He came for them silently. The door slammed open. Irréelle dropped the shovel. The goggles fell forward onto the bridge of Guy's nose. They lost the element of surprise, and before they could charge forward, the watchman swept into the shed and, with his gloved hands, clasped hold of them by their wrists.

He squeezed tight, until Irréelle released the spade and Guy let the rake fall to the ground. Still in his hand, the trowel looked only like a gardening tool, nothing that would hold back the watchman. He dropped that too and shook the goggles from his face.

"I'll be glad to be rid of the two of you. Now, come along."

"Be rid of us?" Irréelle said, fearing whatever horrible punishment the watchman had decided upon.

He pulled them through the door and marched them past the cottage and toward the gate.

Toward Miss Vesper.

Irréelle startled at the sight of her, swept up in a rush of emotions so mangled she could not separate dread from hope.

With small, fast steps, Miss Vesper paced up and down the sidewalk outside the cemetery. And above her, a lone tattletale bat flew through the sky on its four dirt-and-cobweb wings.

Somehow, it must have survived the storm and found its way to Miss Vesper's ear.

Irréelle quavered. She felt like she was falling backward, remembering her very small place in the world—no matter her desire for something more.

The watchman strode forward. "Imagine my surprise when the bell rang at the gate and I received a midnight caller. One so gentle and fine, come to collect the likes of you. Worried sick by her poor lost orphans, she said. I would not be so good as she, taking in what someone else thought fit to abandon."

Irréelle would have much preferred Miss Vesper's sad tale to the truth, and she could almost believe it. Despite the late hour, Miss Vesper looked as neat and tidy as she always did. She wore a thin black jacket over her black dress and her honey-brown hair fell to her shoulders. When she saw Irréelle and Guy, she hurried closer and placed a hand to her chest. Her mouth shaped an O.

Irréelle had never seen that expression cross Miss Vesper's face before. How she had longed for Miss Vesper to gaze upon her with such care, but Irréelle knew it was an act. A pretty mask that veiled her anger. Irréelle stole a look at Guy.

His face was downturned. He shuffled his feet as the watchman walked them over to the gate and unlocked it. It clicked open and the watchman swung back the gate. It shuddered on the hinges.

"Thank you *ever* so much." Miss Vesper's words dripped with sweetness, so thick it made Irréelle's bones ache. She turned to Irréelle and Guy, throwing both arms out in front of her. Despite her air of concern, her icy blue eyes cut straight through Irréelle. "Children." When neither of them moved toward her, she came to them, placing one hand on Irréelle's shoulder and the other on Guy's forearm. Her fingernails dug into their skin, in contrast to her honeyed tone. "You mustn't scare me like that." And then to the watchman, she said, "Thank you again for your trouble."

The fluttering in Irréelle's stomach intensified, her conflicting emotions tumbling all over one another.

Miss Vesper dipped her hand into her purse and passed a wad of bills into the watchman's hand.

The watchman grinned, a slow slide of his lips. "It was no trouble, no trouble at all." He pocketed the money.

Miss Vesper led Irréelle and Guy out of the cemetery and onto the sidewalk. Behind them, the watchman shut the gate. He began to whistle.

23

A Gust of Wind and Dirt

The streetlamps glowed yellow and lit their way past dark-windowed houses. Not a soul stirred, except for the bat overhead.

Miss Vesper took Irréelle by the hand and then she reached for Guy, who had pulled ahead, as if they would otherwise run. Not that they could have. Irréelle moved along, *compelled* by Miss Vesper's will.

A strange sensation, to be sure, but Irréelle marveled more at Miss Vesper's touch. Her palm was cold; her fingers were icy. *They are the fingers of someone who has died*, Irréelle reminded herself. She stole a glance at Miss Vesper, who looked as she always did. No less perfect. No less alive.

Someone both real and unreal.

Miss Vesper's heels clicked on the sidewalk.

"What a reunion we will have," she said to Guy. If Irréelle had heard sweetness in her voice when she spoke to the watchman, it was gone now, replaced with an affected delight. "Wherever were you hiding all this time?"

On the other side of Miss Vesper, Guy walked as far from her as the stretch of their arms would allow. Irréelle could see no more than his profile and his jaw clenched tight.

"And you." Miss Vesper turned to Irréelle. "What a game you played, running off as you did, and with the only candle. I was caught in the dark in that dreadful basement. If it were not for the matches still in my pocket, I might have lost my footing and fallen quite horribly down the stairs." Miss Vesper's smile looked like that of a doll, small and stiff and painted on.

Irréelle sucked in a breath at the reference to the long-ago accident.

She had the suspicion Miss Vesper wanted no one to know her secret and would be most displeased she and Guy had discovered it. Miss Vesper might do anything to protect her secret, even grant Irréelle and Guy their deepest wishes. Or destroy them once and for all.

Each of their footsteps fell out of rhythm of the

others. Quiet and grim, Irréelle stared forlornly at the neighbors' homes. She wondered about the lives within them, so very different from her own. Real mothers and fathers. Real children. What elements were they made of that she was missing?

From the end of the block, Irréelle caught sight of her own home, snug among all the others. Smoke billowed from the two chimneys, the only house that burned a fire in summer. Light blazed in every window, even the small attic window on the third floor. The house looked warm and inviting and . . .

In the attic, a shadow passed in front of the light.

Neither Guy nor Miss Vesper seemed to have noticed, and thank goodness for that. It had to be Lass sneaking about. Irréelle could hardly believe Lass had found a way into the attic, which Miss Vesper locked every time she left it.

Irréelle should have thought of it before, but of any place in the house, in the attic they might find a clue leading not only to the unmarked grave but also to the source of Miss Vesper's magic.

Miss Vesper dropped their hands to open the front gate and herded them through. Once she fastened the lock, she went ahead up the stairs and then gazed down at them from the gabled porch. The dirt-made bat settled in the eaves. "Come inside."

Before he could step away, Irréelle touched a hand to Guy's arm. She did not know when she would have another opportunity to talk to him, and she needed to right things between them. "I'm sorry. I didn't know what to do but give the watchman her name. Please don't be angry with me."

Guy's eyebrows drew together. "But I'm not mad at you."

It was the last thing Irréelle expected to hear. "You're not?"

"I'm the one who got us both caught." He looked down at the ground and then up again. "One way or another we were going to end up back here. You just saved the watchman from having to torture it out of us." His eyes brightened a shade as he said this last remark.

In other circumstances Irréelle might have smiled, but as it was, with Miss Vesper watching, she only nodded. On the inside, her heart swelled.

"I won't leave you, seeing as how you saved me. And you're my friend and all." His cheeks reddened and he hurried on. "I'll help you find the unmarked grave." Guy glanced at Miss Vesper from under his thick brows. "Although it might be our end."

Irréelle placed her foot on the first step. "No, whatever happens, this will not be our end. It will be our beginning."

Side by side, they climbed the wooden steps. Irréelle did not want to reach the top. For these last moments, she could pretend all would be forgiven.

Miss Vesper herded them into the house. "Welcome back." She strode past them and removed her jacket, hanging it in the closet beneath the staircase. Irréelle and Guy locked eyes, at once hopeful and wary, and followed. Catching the look that passed between them, Miss Vesper shook her head. "Oh my. Did you think I was referring to the two of you?"

Irréelle stopped in her tracks. She had, of course, assumed exactly that. Her palms turned sweaty. It felt suddenly overwarm in the entryway. Through the double doors to the study, the fire roared in the hearth.

"Come," Miss Vesper said.

In Irréelle's pocket, the Hand fidgeted. A moment later, it slipped out and ran along her arm, which she raised in front of her. She was not surprised or disappointed, or really anything at all, other than accepting. She knew what it was like to have no choices.

"*Come*," Miss Vesper said more firmly. The Hand

jumped from Irréelle's arm to the banister. Miss Vesper patted it once and smiled. "Now, off you go." The Hand leapt to the ground, landing nimbly, then it circled around Irréelle's ankles, untied one of Guy's bootlaces, and darted into the study.

Guy took a step back. Though her legs trembled, Irréelle was determined to stay where she was.

The weight of Miss Vesper's gaze pressed into Irréelle. "The boy said something that caught my interest. That you saved the watchman from having to punish you."

"His name is Guy," Irréelle whispered. She did not correct Miss Vesper's other error. If she recalled, Guy had used the word *torture*. She swallowed hard.

Miss Vesper went on, as if she had not heard Irréelle. "Well, now the pleasure will be mine."

Irréelle wanted to back away, but still did not move, Guy's words offering her strength. *More brave, more strange, more stubborn.*

A frown settled onto Miss Vesper's face. "You did not even bother to wipe your boots."

Irréelle would have thought it an odd thing to mention, something insignificant when dirt clung to every inch of them, if she did not know Miss Vesper so well. She itched to brush off her skirt or straighten her hair, but all she said was, "I'm sorry." But for the first time, she did not mean it.

Miss Vesper stepped closer to Irréelle. She lifted her hand as if she was about to stroke her cheek, but then she thrust it forward, palm out. Her eyes narrowed to slits.

A gust of wind and dirt rushed over Irréelle's face and swept through the entryway. It tickled the backs of her knees and rippled her skirt, swirling up from the floor, spinning around her, soft at first and then twisting faster. Her hair lashed across her cheeks. The crystal prisms dangling from the body of the chandelier tinkled.

It felt like she stood in the center of a storm. The dirt scratched like sandpaper on the exposed parts of her skin. Pressure built around her. Wind shrieked in her ears.

Guy's hair whipped across his face as the dirt and wind twisted through the strands and blew across his scalp. The wind scraped dust and dirt from their skin. It whirled in a cloud around them.

Miss Vesper strained to control it. Though she stood very still with her feet set together, her arms shook. The color rose in her cheeks. They flushed pink. Her hair lifted from her shoulders and tossed in the air.

Beneath their feet the floor vibrated. Miss Vesper pushed her hands forward. Her brow drew together. One finger at a time, she curled her hands into fists. When she raised her arms above her head, the dirt gathered in the air. It churned like a storm cloud.

Irréelle blinked dust from her eyes.

And then Miss Vesper opened her hands again, fingers spread wide. She shaped the dirt into a dark blade.

It sliced through the air.

24

A Terrible Mistake

Irréelle ducked and yanked Guy down beside her. The dirt-made knife spun end over end, clipping off the very tips of his tousled hair.

Guy patted his body, as if to make sure everything was still attached. Irréelle felt faint. If she had not grabbed him in time, he might have lost his head.

But there was still a chance he would.

The knife swung round, making a perfect arc through the air and slashing low. Irréelle darted right and Guy leapt to the left.

The blade cut through the sliver of space between them, snipping the hem of Irréelle's dress. A mangled strip of fabric held on by a thread.

"Be still." Miss Vesper's words fell sharp-edged and absolute. Her hands clutched at the air, as if she manipulated its very consistency.

Irréelle froze. An itchy, demanding force kept her in place. Across the entryway, Guy's body stiffened. His face scrunched up, his arms shook, struggling against Miss Vesper's magical command.

The dirt-made knife flashed above his head, taking another hank of hair.

"Don't hurt him," Irréelle said, finding strength to defend him even though she was so unused to doing so for herself.

Miss Vesper waved her arm through the air, and the knife swerved. It charged in Irréelle's direction.

"Stop!" She spoke before the blade stole her voice. Whatever half life she had, it was better than none at all. She did not want it cut short. "You are making a terrible mistake."

Miss Vesper's eyebrow spiked. The knife swept through the air, faster and faster. Unable to move more than a few inches despite how she strained, Irréelle stared it down.

Closer and closer.

It angled for her throat.

"Irréelle!" Guy cringed, watching everything unfold

through squinted eyes, as if to prepare himself for her gruesome beheading.

The knife was within inches of striking her.

Desperate, Irréelle shouted, "We can help you with the *other* task!"

Just as the blade pressed against skin—it stopped in midair.

Miss Vesper's hand wavered. The dirt-made knife dropped to the floor and disintegrated into a pile of earth and dust.

Irréelle and Guy stood on wobbly legs, their will returned to them. She brushed her fingers across her neck, wet with the thinnest line of blood.

Every part of her tingled, the nerves on the very surface of her skin icy where Miss Vesper's magic had touched. She slipped closer to Guy, that feeling rushing through her again, that she was small and insubstantial. Her arm brushed against his, and their knocking elbows at least reassured her she was solid.

Miss Vesper lowered her arms, fingers twitching, and rolled back her shoulders, everything about her appearance just-off. Her bright eyes darkened and the finest blue veins ran beneath her skin, almost translucent across her sharpened bones. She smoothed down her hair, which had gone quite wild and lost its luster.

"Why would I need your help when I've already created your replacement?" Even her voice was not quite her own. Somehow, the dark magic plucked at her light and beauty. It drained her, Irréelle realized, if only temporarily. Miss Vesper twisted her ring, looser now on her skinny-boned finger. "A replacement much more competent and clever than either of you." Guy opened his mouth, but Irréelle spoke over him, not trusting what he would say. Something to stir things up, she was sure, and they were already in enough trouble. Now was the time for her to be brave, to stand up to Miss Vesper the way she should have done all along.

"We are not something to discard when you grow tired of us." It felt good to speak the words, to believe them, even if they would never sway Miss Vesper. Irréelle tried to channel Lass, who seemed not to have a single bone of self-doubt in her body. She bared everything she had to Miss Vesper. "We are very close to finding the unmarked grave." She may have exaggerated, but knew the offer must be strong or Miss Vesper would dismiss her without consideration.

Miss Vesper gripped the banister, steadying herself. "Tell me what you've found."

Irréelle's heart raced as fast as hummingbird wings. "I

won't," she said. "Not until you promise something for each of us in return. Whatever it is we want."

"What has gotten into you?" Miss Vesper released the railing. She came closer and stared down her nose at Irréelle. "And what is it *you* want?"

The words stuck in Irréelle's throat. It took everything in her to dislodge them. "For you to magic me real."

Miss Vesper's lip twitched. "Such a silly thing you are."

"Please, Miss Vesper," Irréelle said, sounding less like Lass and more like herself.

"You are bluffing. I will burn your bones to ashes and be done with you and the boy."

She spoke with such certainty that Irréelle shook with fright. Miss Vesper would snuff them out of existence.

Unless Irréelle poked at the place where Miss Vesper was most tender.

It was the same spot where Irréelle felt most vulnerable. Her heart. For it held Guy and Lass within its chambers, and she refused to be parted from them. "Imagine us away and you will be alone forever." Irréelle lowered her voice. "You will never see the one you love again. Burn our bones and what we know will burn with us."

Miss Vesper's features contorted, eyes shining with malice. She raised her hand.

Guy nudged Irréelle to the side. "There is something wrong with your face," he said to Miss Vesper. His upper lip curled back as if he found the sight of her most distasteful.

"How dare you!" Miss Vesper crossed the distance between them in two strides and slapped Guy across the face. Her ring, already so loose, flew off her finger and clattered to the ground.

Guy stumbled backward, tripping over his untied bootlace. He glared at Miss Vesper, who looked at her finger as if she could not believe the ring no longer circled it.

Irréelle dropped to her knees and fumbled for the ring. It weighed almost nothing when she lifted it from the floor and tipped it to the light. She had seen the flash of its diamond so many times, only never this close. It sparkled like the brightest star. Yet it was not the glittering stone that hypnotized her but the golden band and the words inscribed in the metal. They tangled together like the most delicate tree branches.

❤ *Like a hawthorn, fair blooms my love.* ❤

She lost her breath. The inscription mirrored the lines from Miss Vesper's gravestone. Or they almost did.

Something was different, but Irréelle had no time for reflection just then.

Miss Vesper's shadow fell across Irréelle's bent form. "Give it back at once or I will pry it from your fingers."

Irréelle scrambled to her feet, as careful with the ring as she would be with the flame of a candle. Something she should not touch. She placed the ring on Miss Vesper's outstretched palm.

With a shaking hand, Miss Vesper slipped it over her knuckle.

Irréelle moved closer to Guy. "Are you all right?"

"Didn't hurt," he said out the side of his mouth, but Irréelle knew he would not admit if it had.

"You truly are little monsters." Miss Vesper touched her ring, a sure sign she was thinking of N.M.H., perhaps recalling the promises they had made to each other long ago.

"After all I've taught you of obedience, look at the disgraceful way you behave." Miss Vesper's eyes narrowed, as if she could peer into Irréelle's mind and snatch up the truth. "But maybe you have more inside your head than cobwebs. Find me the unmarked grave, and quickly." Miss Vesper's mouth pinched. "But one misstep will seal your fate. Do you understand?"

"I do," Irréelle said. With her uneven bones, missteps were the only kind she could make.

25

A Good Cup of Tea

The idea would not settle in her head, that Irréelle had spoken her mind, that she had convinced Miss Vesper to spare her, and Guy as well. She very much felt like smiling, but schooled her features as best she could.

"I am parched. Fetch me some tea." Miss Vesper touched her ring as she strode into the study.

Irréelle and Guy exchanged a look.

"Get it yourself," he muttered.

She hushed him, not wanting to give Miss Vesper a reason to change her mind. Irréelle grabbed hold of Guy's arm and dragged him down the hall.

In the kitchen doorway, they stopped short. Somehow,

Lass was already there, still wrapped in her coat and pacing on silent feet.

"What's going on?" she asked.

"Tea," Irréelle said. "And quickly."

Lass filled a kettle with water and set it on the stove. "Next time I'm eavesdropping, please speak up. I could barely hear a thing."

"How did you get downstairs without us seeing you?" Guy found a mug in the cupboard and placed it on the counter.

"How did you *not* see me?" Lass smiled.

"Not that one." Irréelle pushed aside the mug Guy had chosen, then reached past him and selected the delicate bone china teacup and saucer. "This one is Miss Vesper's favorite."

Guy shook his head as if he could not tell one from the other.

Irréelle traced the pattern along the edge of the saucer. "Were you in the attic? I thought I saw a shadow pass the window."

Lass nodded. "Miss Vesper must have left in such a hurry she forgot to lock the door."

Miss Vesper had never before been so careless. The

attic was always kept tight as a vault when she was not in it. She must have been in such a rush to reach the graveyard.

"Oh my." Irréelle would have run up the stairs and sneaked through the door if she did not already know Miss Vesper would catch her.

Irréelle longed to pore over the journals that filled the bookcases. She had only ever glimpsed their pages when Miss Vesper cracked them open on the table. The handwriting looped across the paper, a much finer script than Miss Vesper's own tightly crunched letters. And Miss Vesper referred to them so frequently and guarded them so fiercely, Irréelle knew they must hold secrets. Within them, she might find magical words or a bone dust spell that would make her real. "What did you find?"

"Not what I was looking for." Lass squeezed past them.

Irréelle wondered what, exactly, Lass had hoped to find, but did not pry.

"Nothing about N.M.H.?" Guy bent to tie his bootlace.

"There wasn't enough time." Lass lifted the kettle, shook it, and then returned it to the stove. The water sloshed side to side.

"I learned something," Irréelle said, before disappointment could sink in. They all turned their heads toward the empty doorway as if Miss Vesper might have been hovering there, listening, and then they huddled closer. "Miss Vesper's ring fell off," she explained to Lass. "And I retrieved it for her."

"Yes, yes. That is when I slipped downstairs." She grinned at Guy. "And when I slipped the notebook from the pocket of Miss Vesper's dress."

"I can't believe it," Guy said, but he too was smiling, as impressed as Irréelle.

"We can look through it later. Tell us what you've found," Lass said.

Irréelle wanted to pore over the notebook right then, but they did not have enough time, so she continued. "The ring was engraved. It said something like, *fair blooms my love.* The words were all wound up with hearts and leafy branches." *Like the design on Miss Vesper's headstone.*

"Oh!" Lass exclaimed, and then slapped the ends of her too-long sleeves over her mouth.

"Miss Vesper and N.M.H. must not only be in love . . ." Irréelle clasped her hands and held them in front of her chest, directly over her heart. "They must also be *engaged.* And he leaves hearts for her everywhere. Maybe one will also lead us to his grave."

A sharp, high-pitched whistle issued from the kettle, and Irréelle jumped. Lass snatched it from the stove with the cuff of her coat, and the hissing trailed off.

Irréelle straightened the hem of her dress. "First . . ." She sprinkled tea leaves into the cup and held it out, nudging Lass to pour. "I will bring Miss Vesper her tea. You two stay here." They had already made her wait too long.

With that, she spun on her heel and returned to the study. When she entered the room, Miss Vesper sat at her desk before the open window. Darkness leaked in, lengthening the lines on her pale face. The Hand perched on the desktop in front of her, raised up on its five fingers.

"Be still," Miss Vesper said. The Hand went rigid, knuckles straining. "Be *still*." It swayed on its fingertips and then collapsed in a heap. Miss Vesper lifted its limp form and tossed it into a drawer.

Irréelle averted her eyes so Miss Vesper did not see the flint sharpening her gaze. "Here is your tea." She set the cup down on the desk and scooped in an overflowing spoonful of bone dust. When Miss Vesper did not immediately reach for it, Irréelle added another dash.

"I'd almost forgotten how accommodating you could be." Miss Vesper lifted the teacup with both hands and drank down the scalding liquid. Breath steamed from her mouth when she spoke. "Delicious."

As a smile slid across Miss Vesper's face, color bloomed

in her cheeks, and shiny streaks of gold slipped from the roots to the tips of her hair. The flesh on her bones plumped up, and she sat straighter in the chair.

Irréelle felt the strangest tug in her bones, as if she were no more than a speck of dust Miss Vesper could call forth or send away. Without intending to, she found herself leaning forward.

Miss Vesper looked at her with wild eyes, quite in contrast to the words she spoke next. "You do make a good cup of tea. In fact, you should try it."

Irréelle shook her head, unsure what trick Miss Vesper might be playing. "No, thank you."

"Oh, perhaps you would prefer it sweeter. I have just the thing." Miss Vesper reached into the pocket of her skirt and extracted a small vial, swirling with a dark liquid. She uncapped the cork and poured three drops into the teacup, and then three more.

Still, Irréelle hesitated.

"I insist." Miss Vesper offered a smile that softened the look of her hollow-cheeked face. "Would you pass up an opportunity for longevity? For *life*?" She shrugged one narrow shoulder, dangling the possibility but making no promises.

Irréelle clasped on to Miss Vesper's words, bright

with hope. She accepted the cup, the tea shades darker now. It smelled of mint, just as it always did. Although she had stolen a taste once before, perhaps she had not had *enough*.

She took a sip, careful not to burn her tongue. Vanilla mingled with peppermint, but it could not mask the bitter taste of bone dust.

And disappointment.

There was no spark of magic. Nothing to liven her like a true flesh-and-bone girl. She wanted no more of the tea and false hopes.

Before Irréelle could lower it, Miss Vesper placed one finger on the bottom of the cup and forced the rest of the contents down her throat. Irréelle sputtered and coughed.

"Best I have some insurance," Miss Vesper said, retrieving the cup from Irréelle's shaking hands.

"What do you mean?" Irréelle took a step back, mistrustful of the way Miss Vesper's eyes darkened.

"Have patience."

Only Irréelle did not have to wait long. A prickling sensation coursed through her body. A gentle nudging, a blurring and slowing of her thoughts.

"No," she said, her voice as thin as a thread. Too late, she realized what Miss Vesper had done.

Six drops, not of vanilla, but of Miss Vesper's serum for insomnia. Much too much for someone as small as Irréelle.

Fatigue weighted her limbs. Though she struggled to keep them open, her eyelids slipped closed.

She fell to the floor, lost to darkness.

26

The Source of Magic

Irréelle tossed and turned, caught in a fitful slumber. Her mind stirred up dreams of darkness and emptiness, a vast expanse of nothing from which she might never escape. When at last she clawed her way to wakefulness, the sun sat at the horizon. It glowed orange through the bedroom window.

Disoriented, she put a hand to her head. And then it all flooded back, how Miss Vesper had laced the tea with sleeping serum and forced it down Irréelle's throat.

A bitter taste sat on her tongue, as distasteful as Miss Vesper's deceit. Maybe Irréelle should have been used to it, but it ached like a fresh wound. Miss Vesper would always do what she wanted.

And it was time for Irréelle to do the same.

She sprang out of bed, staggering across her room on sleep-heavy legs, and caught herself against the door. The wood groaned and she waited a beat, listening to the quiet before twisting the knob. Only it would not open.

She pulled and yanked, but it refused to turn no matter how much she rattled it.

Irréelle should have expected this too. The locked door seemed as impenetrable as Miss Vesper's heart. She could not force her way through either barrier no matter how desperately she wished it.

All the hope she held inside crimped at the edges. Her friends had believed her idea would work, that all might be well. And she had failed them.

Holding back tears, she shook the doorknob again.

From the hallway came the patter of footsteps. Her hand dropped to her side.

She lifted her chin, preparing herself for another confrontation with Miss Vesper.

"Shh," a voice hissed, one that nearly made her collapse in relief.

Irréelle bent her face to the keyhole. Lass's dark eye stared back at her.

"You've been asleep for ages," Lass said. "I've been

worried and wondering if you'd ever wake."

"And Guy?"

"Oh, he's all right. But mad as can be at Miss Vesper."

"The door is locked," Irréelle said, as if there must be some mistake.

"Of course it is," Lass whispered. "Miss Vesper won't let you out except to do her bidding. And with you locked up, she knows Guy won't dash either. She's told us we're to continue searching for the grave and collecting bone dust."

Miss Vesper will always do what she wants. And it was something Irréelle would never again forget.

"She won't honor our agreement. Not if she's having you collect bone dust." Irréelle thought saying it aloud would frighten her, but instead, knowing Miss Vesper intended to replace them bolstered Irréelle. "She will break every promise she's made."

Lass's eye squinted as if she was thinking over the lies Miss Vesper had told her. "What should we do?"

"It's up to us now." Irréelle held the thought close. *Us.* She was not alone. "We have to find the source of Miss Vesper's magic."

Light glinted in Lass's dark eye. "That sounds like more fun anyway."

"In the meantime, we must do as she tells us. We don't want her to suspect anything."

"Guy and I can't do everything," Lass said, a smile in her voice. "You have to keep yourself good and busy too."

A moment later, something slid under the door, nudging up against the tips of Irréelle's boots.

Miss Vesper's notebook.

Irréelle did not have a key to the door, but perhaps this book held the key to accessing magic. She lifted it carefully, wanting to be respectful of Miss Vesper's privacy as much as she wanted to tear back the pages and read it all at once. "Have you read it?"

"I couldn't make sense of it, not her ramblings about bone dust and the unmarked grave. And definitely not the mushy poem."

"A poem?" It did not seem like something Miss Vesper would write. Irréelle looked down at the notebook. It was plain and black on each side, giving no hint as to which was the front and which was the back.

"Maybe you will have better luck with it." Lass's voice came muffled, as if she had angled away from the door. Irréelle snugged her eye to the keyhole again. A flash of Lass's hair swept past as she turned away. When her eye reappeared, it was rounded in alarm. "I've got to run."

The clicking of Miss Vesper's heels on the metal staircase shook the door in its frame.

"Wait." Irréelle pressed her face to the wood, but Lass was already gone, ducking fast into the shadows.

Irréelle leaned back against the door, clutching the notebook until Miss Vesper passed by. And then she opened it.

(She was only a little disappointed when magic did not immediately snap at her fingertips or ripple on the page.)

She sat there for many hours, reading each and every line and finding that all Lass had said was true. Few of Miss Vesper's jottings and notations about magic made sense. And the comments Irréelle could understand, she found quite troubling.

Their bodies take shape, but they are mindless things, filled only with my imaginings. A drop of my blood. They are no more than bony puppets.

Irréelle's hand clenched when she read these lines, crinkling the corner of the page. Miss Vesper's blood ran in her veins. Such a small amount, but enough to tether them. Enough to give Miss Vesper control of Irréelle's movements when they were near each other.

But worse scribblings followed.

*Heads filled with cobwebs. I must brush them away, wipe clean their will, and capture it for my own. One command and they are done for. *Simple creatures.*

227

It seemed to confirm all Irréelle had feared—how little effort it would take for Miss Vesper to turn bones to dust.

But the magic itself eluded Irréelle.

Deflated, she reached the last page. The words ran across the paper upside down. She flipped the notebook around. Whereas the other pages ran thick with ink, here there were only a few brief lines, written in a hand other than Miss Vesper's.

It must have been the poem Lass had mentioned, for Irréelle had seen formulas and ingredients and a great many ramblings in the rest of the notebook, but never anything resembling a poem.

She skimmed the neatly penned words. Irréelle could not be sure, as she had only ever glimpsed the pages when Miss Vesper referred to the journals, but she thought it was written by N.M.H.

Irréelle read it again, searching the words for a clue.

Breathe of the wind
& with it soar
fair skies
Hush still the night

rest evermore thine eyes

It had the same tone as the words on Miss Vesper's headstone but otherwise made little sense to Irréelle. She had never seen Miss Vesper *fly*, of that she was certain. Maybe it was meant as a lullaby, as Miss Vesper had such trouble sleeping. Or perhaps it was some sort of goodbye.

She closed the journal and thought over what next to do.

After all she had read, she was more certain than ever that Miss Vesper would not honor their agreement. Irréelle would have to find a way into the attic and uncover the original source of magic.

She needed to read N.M.H.'s journals.

* * *

Much later, in the darkest part of the night, long after Guy and Lass had left for the cemetery on some false hunt and after Miss Vesper retired to her room (hopefully with serum-infused tea), Irréelle reached under her bed. She was not sure if she would find her box or if Miss Vesper had thrown it away, so when her fingers brushed its edge, she smiled.

With both hands, she dragged the box toward her and pulled off the lid. Inside, the feather lay where she had left it. She plucked it with her fingertips and stood, but tonight she would not use it to measure her height.

Instead, Irréelle slipped it into the keyhole, jiggling it about until the lock, amazingly and wonderfully, clicked. She peeked out the door and looked both ways down the darkened hallway. At the far end, Miss Vesper's door stood closed. Irréelle tiptoed in the opposite direction, stopping at the base of the spiral staircase.

Nothing looked different, but everything felt different, as if Miss Vesper breathed beside her, a pulse in the air where she had fallen to her death all those years ago. Irréelle swept her hand through the air to calm it and skirted around the floorboards.

But she could not leave behind the lingering, creeping feeling that Miss Vesper would awaken, aware that something was amiss. She did not even want to *think* Miss Vesper's name, fearful that thoughts alone might summon her.

Step by step, Irréelle wound up the staircase, imagining she could walk as swiftly as Lass and go unnoticed. She placed her feet lightly so the soles made almost no sound on the metal.

At the top, she glanced the long way down and listened. Everything remained quiet.

Irréelle turned to the attic door and twisted the knob. The lock rattled, and the springs twanged in protest, refusing to open. Lifting the feather, she fitted it in the keyhole. The sharp spine did not bend or break, but rubbed against the lock's internal workings. For many minutes, she poked and prodded. The old lock, larger and sturdier and more complex than the one fitted to her bedroom door, groaned, but it would not budge.

Her shoulders sagged, and she slumped against the railing at the top of the staircase. All the answers she needed lay on the other side of the door, but they may as well have been across the world, for Irréelle could not reach them.

The feather fell from her hand, drifting to the floor far below. It made no sound, but Irréelle alighted down the stairs, as if its gentle landing might rouse Miss Vesper from her slumber.

At the bottom of the staircase, she snatched up the feather, eyes darting toward Miss Vesper's door again.

Still closed. Still quiet.

And the feather in her hand, still useless.

There had to be another way. One that did not involve

sneaking into Miss Vesper's room and stealing the key to the attic. The very thought of it froze Irréelle in place. Her bones would not let her do something so foolish.

She did not want to admit defeat but could think of no way *into* the attic, just as there had been no way *out* of the watchman's shed. Except he had taunted them, had he not? By alluding to a skeleton key, able to finesse any lock.

But she did not even know if such a thing existed.

Unless.

Unless it was a different sort of key, true to its name— not crafted from iron or brass, but instead, forged from the bones of a skeleton.

Tucked in the shadows under the spiral staircase, Irréelle grinned.

She knew where to find a good many bones.

27

The Skeleton Key

The bone garden awaited Irréelle's return.

Candle in hand, she slipped down the darkened passageways, taking careful steps so as not to wake some dormant magic and alert the dirt-made bats to her presence. A few of them must have remained, lost in the tunnels or keeping watch for Miss Vesper. She heard the whisper of their wings around every corner. A hushed murmuring that grew louder the deeper she ventured into the underside of the graveyard.

She edged away from the strange echo of their movements, intent on finding a skeleton key and willing to let the bats be.

But the sounds drifted closer, as if the little beasts sought her out.

Irréelle's heart sped in her chest. She turned and she ran.

Not away, but straight toward them, gathering up a rock as she tore down the passageway. Oh, those bats were asking for trouble.

Ahead, shapes shifted in the shadows. A light flickered. Irréelle cranked back her arm and then let the rock fly.

It landed with a thud.

"Hey!" a voice shouted.

"Guy?" Irréelle crept forward, holding out her candle. "What are you doing down here?"

Lass stepped around the corner, swinging an oil lamp turned down so low it cast more shadow than light. "We're looking for clues."

"Did Miss Vesper let you out?" Guy asked, rubbing his shoulder.

"Not exactly," Irréelle said. "But never mind all that. I've thought of what we must do."

And then she told them her plan.

"A skeleton key," Lass said, striding ahead of them, the long sleeves of her coat swishing at her sides. "Why didn't I think of that?"

"How will we find one?" Guy dragged his feet, eyes on the ceiling, as if he imagined it collapsing on him again.

Not just any bone would do, but Irréelle had little idea how to find the right one. "I don't know."

"We'll ask the bones, of course," Lass said. "There must be a locksmith among them."

"What do you mean, 'we'll ask the bones'? They aren't going to sit up and have a conversation with us." Guy stalked forward, seeming to push past his fear of the tunnels in favor of bickering with Lass. "You probably want to invite them to the study for tea too."

"Don't be silly," she said. "Skeletons don't drink tea."

But Irréelle was still focused on Lass's first comment, thinking back to her time in the above side of the graveyard. "I saw a headstone." They turned back, too far ahead of the candlelight for her to see more than their shadowed outlines in the glow of the lantern. "For a locksmith."

"Well, why didn't you say so?" Lass grinned. "Which way?"

Irréelle tried to orient herself. "That way?" she said uncertainly, pointing toward a tunnel strung with cobwebs.

Lass closed her eyes for a moment, face twisted in concentration, and then they flashed open. "Yes!" She tugged Irréelle down the narrow passageway, swiping spiderwebs out of the way with the sleeve of her coat. Guy came grumbling after them. "Feel that?" Lass asked.

Irréelle listened to the bones. She heard their familiar hum and their unique rhythms, but she could not distinguish them clearly enough to know a locksmith from any of the others. "I don't—"

"Think of silver keys and sturdy locks," Lass said.

"How about a rusted lock and a long-lost key?" Guy crept up from behind. "And a body wasting away in a dungeon."

"No, no," Lass said. "That won't work at all."

"Heavy chains and iron locks?" Guy went on. "To weight a body thrown into the ocean."

"No more nonsense." Lass slashed her arm through the air as if to wipe away his words. "Focus on the locksmith and his tools. Think of who he might have been." She glared at Guy.

"Someone crafty and smart—" His mouth hung open as if he intended to say more, but Lass interrupted.

"Stop there, before you ruin it." Guy clenched his jaw and Lass continued. "Someone quiet and patient, who understood the language of locks."

"Someone with nimble fingers," Irréelle said, remembering the inscription on the tombstone.

"Yes!" Lass exclaimed.

Irréelle tuned in to the bones, sifting through their different tones. And then she felt everything click ever so gently. "I feel *something*," she said.

She looked at Guy expectantly. He shrugged, probably too stubborn to admit Lass was right. "I guess."

"So noisy and impatient." Lass passed the lantern to Guy and sped up. "We're coming, we're coming."

They took a few more turns, jogging to keep up with Lass, and then she slipped out of sight. "Bring the light." Her voice came from the darkness.

Irréelle walked forward, and Guy wedged into the small alcove beside her. Before them lay a wooden coffin engraved with tiny keys, and within it rested the locksmith.

Guy sucked in a deep breath, as if the enclosed space was much too small for his liking. Irréelle handed him the candle. The flame cast a shaky shadow on the wall as she knelt in the dirt before the casket. "Hello," she said to the skeleton. "Will you allow us to borrow a bone?"

"Oh, he doesn't mind. Take a finger bone," Lass said.

"Are you sure?" Guy asked, frowning at the lantern and candle he had been forced to carry.

"I know what my bones know," Lass said. "I'm sure."

And Irréelle felt it too. The locksmith's nimble

fingers would have crafted countless keys and bypassed the most intricate of locks.

She reached out, her hand hovering over the skeleton. She let the gentle tugging in her palm guide her and plucked up a pinkie bone. It was a grayish white, knobby at the ends, and skinny as could be. The perfect size for a keyhole.

* * *

Once they returned to the house, they wound their way up the spiral staircase. Lass tiptoed as quiet as a shadow. Behind her, Irréelle clutched the skeleton key. And Guy climbed up after them, all the better to keep watch for Miss Vesper (or so he said).

For the first time, Irréelle was no longer facing the world on her own. Her loneliness, which she had always held so close, crept away.

"What are you waiting for?" Lass asked, bouncing on her toes and somehow managing not to make a sound. "Open it, open it, open it."

Irréelle turned to the door. Lass squeezed in close on her right and Guy pressed in from the left. She slid the bone into the keyhole and twisted.

The lock clicked open. Irréelle said a silent thank-you to the bone.

She nodded at Guy and Lass. *Together*, they would search for the secrets to magic. And together, they might change their fates.

One hand to the door, Irréelle pushed, cracking it just wide enough for them to pass through. Once Guy shut the door behind them, they grinned at each other, and then their eyes swept around the attic.

"Look how high up we are." Lass gazed out the octagonal window that faced the backyard.

Irréelle came up beside her, pushing to her toes and looking down. She had never seen the yard from this angle before. They peered at the treetops and the path of stepping stones evenly spaced through the overgrown grass between them. Something about the misshapen stones reminded Irréelle of the underside of the graveyard. She squinted, but it was simply too dark to make out more than their vague outline, so she turned, pushing away thoughts of those dark passageways.

Moonlight filtered through the skylights and fell in pale lines across the worktable. The jars and vials, the mortar and pestle, the spoons and scalpel, all sat in their proper places. Irréelle set Miss Vesper's journal in the middle of the table, where it was caught in a moonbeam.

She could not rightfully keep what did not belong to

her, and she felt a smidge guilty for reading it at all (especially when it revealed so little). But bit by bit, the guilt faded as she crossed the room and ran her fingers across the notebooks in the bookcases.

There were so many.

Irréelle set down the skeleton key and pulled out the first volume. Guy and Lass came closer.

"Go ahead," Lass said.

Irréelle took a deep breath and then turned to the opening page.

Dr. Nicholas Montgomery Hauser.

A shiver ran through her. N.M.H. After all this time, at last she knew what the initials stood for, who Miss Vesper longed for.

"What does it say?" Guy asked.

She whispered the name aloud, wondering if Dr. Hauser could hear her. If he tossed in his grave, thinking of Miss Vesper.

"Did you say doctor?"

"Like a mad scientist?" Lass asked.

Irréelle looked down at the notebook in her hands. She could not understand the shorthand, but certain words she knew quite well. *Cranium. Tibia. Radius.* "I think he was a bone doctor."

Lass sat cross-legged on the floor and pulled a different journal into her lap. "I wonder what he has to say about bone dust."

"We should look at one of his final journals," Guy suggested, pulling the very last notebook from the shelf. "Everyone knows the end of a story is the very best part." He set it on the table and opened it randomly.

Irréelle's mouth dropped open. The same hand must have written the looping script, but whereas each entry in the first notebook fit neatly on the page, in this book, ink marked the margins and dark lines slashed through huge sections. Cramped words squished above them.

"I can't understand a thing. Can you?" Guy said, tilting his head from side to side. "Maybe he did go a little mad."

Irréelle frowned at the page. "Not mad. Heartsick." Most of the terms and language confused her as well, and she could not read the crossed-out portions, but here and there, underlined notations jumped out at her. "It's a record of his experiments." Irréelle touched her fingertips to the words. "His formulas for bringing Miss Vesper to life."

Guy's eyes widened. "Let's see if we can figure them out."

"Okay," Irréelle said cautiously. Her pulse skipped

expectant and fast. All the answers she needed might rest in these words. If only she could interpret them.

She flipped a page and then another, flattening a corner that had folded over. Peeking out from beneath her finger, marked in fresher ink, someone had jotted two words. She slid her hand away.

*Simple creatures?

It was the same notation Irréelle had seen in Miss Vesper's journal. In fact, it very much looked as if it had been written by Miss Vesper here too, set right beside Dr. Hauser's findings.

A heart that beats and a brain that thinks, such is life complete.

Irréelle wished she knew what it was that prompted Miss Vesper to ponder on simple creatures next to this line when they contrasted each other so completely. Irréelle was about to refer to the little black journal again for comparison when she recalled one of Miss Vesper's notations.

One command and they are done for.

Miss Vesper must have wanted to create something less complex than Dr. Hauser, something she could better control. Like the Hand, a simpler creature without heart or brain. *Be still*, all Miss Vesper had to say for it to collapse. Could it be that Miss Vesper was unable to control Irréelle and her friends in this manner? A tremulous hope surrounded her, too fragile to voice.

"Is there anything about the unmarked grave?" Guy asked, interrupting her thoughts.

"Not that I have seen," Irréelle said. In truth, she had not been thinking of the unmarked grave at all, only of finding the source of the magic.

"Let me have a look." Guy angled Dr. Hauser's journal in his direction.

"It's like reading a book of nonsense," Lass said from the floor. She licked a finger and turned the page. "That mushy poem is in here again. And listen to this. 'Recited by a true heart, love blooms welcome and love gentles farewell.'" She repeated the final word, drawing it out soft and ghostlike. "Farewell."

"Be cautious," Irréelle warned, unsure what might call forth the magic. She did not want Lass to disappear before her eyes.

But nothing at all happened.

"No, no, this is better," Guy said. He poked his finger to the script. "'Red, red blood transforms bones and from the dirt new life groans.'"

"Gross," Lass muttered.

"See what else you can find," Irréelle said.

243

They all bent their heads over separate journals, reading silently for many minutes. Irréelle memorized all she could, the words like a lifeline.

Cinnamon quickens the pulse. And five pages later: *Love sparks the heart.*

Dr. Hauser wrote frequently of love. As if it might be the most important element of magic. She found the word again, on the next page.

"Look," Irréelle said, and then read aloud so Lass, still seated on the floor, could hear as well. "'I will rest, unmarked by regret or grave—'"

The floorboards creaked. Irréelle lifted her eyes from the notebook.

Miss Vesper stood in the doorway. Her blue eyes pierced the moonlit room, as bright as distant stars.

"Oh, do not stop there," she said, words spiking the night.

Irréelle could not speak. Her throat closed up. Beside her, Guy froze, and at her feet, Lass pinched Irréelle's leg.

"Have you lost your voice? Then I shall finish it for you." Miss Vesper closed her eyes and recited the lines from the journal. "'I will rest, unmarked by regret or grave, very clearly marked by love.'"

Irréelle hung on the words. *Yes, of course,* she thought, as the pieces of a complicated puzzle began to come together in her mind. But in the next moment, her thoughts scattered.

Miss Vesper's eyes flashed open and she took a slow step forward.

28

The Shape of Things

The air quivered with energy. All the bones in Irréelle's body tingled and they ached to move forward.

"Did you think you would go undiscovered? Try as you might to be quiet, I can always hear the cracking of your bones." Miss Vesper held up her hand and tugged on invisible strings, calling Irréelle to her. "You have tested my patience."

Irréelle resisted, straining to hold still bones that no longer wanted to obey. "We were only trying to help."

Miss Vesper's face darkened. At her back, vials clattered in the racks and lines splintered their length. She bowed her head, jaw clenched tight. The vials shattered all at once. Bone dust and glass burst forth.

Uncontrolled, it swirled around Miss Vesper, faster and faster. Her hair flapped behind her. Shards of glass nicked her skin.

Tempering her rage, she sucked in a breath. When she released it, everything crashed down, shuddering with such force that pieces of broken glass gouged the floor.

"*Come.*" A jolt thudded in Irréelle's chest, as if Miss Vesper had snatched hold of her ribs and *pulled.*

Guy lurched around the side of the table. He must have felt it too, the most delicate thread tugging him toward Miss Vesper. His boots crunched over the glass. And sitting at Irréelle's feet, Lass began to rise.

Irréelle struggled against the tether and managed to regain control just long enough to press her hand to Lass's shoulder, holding her there in the shadows. "Keep down," Irréelle hissed between clenched teeth. If Miss Vesper had not seen her and was not tugging her forth, there was no reason for Lass to expose herself.

Lass frowned but remained huddled out of sight. At least one of them would be safe.

Another twinge rocked through Irréelle. She staggered around the table like her body was not her own. *I am something more than a simple creature*, she reminded herself. *I have a heart that beats wild and a brain full of thoughts.* If only her body could rebel as much as her heart.

Her feet clomped unevenly, more so than usual. All the while, Miss Vesper stared her down, pupils dark as pits. Purple circles formed under her eyes as she commanded Irréelle closer.

Irréelle tensed her limbs, slowing but not stopping her progression. Guy jerked forward, grumbling and sour-faced. In this manner Miss Vesper led them out of the attic and down, down, down the stairs.

When they reached the first-floor landing, Miss Vesper turned to them. Her face caught both light and shadow, giving her features a strange imbalance. "If you only came when I asked, I would not have to impose my will." She fanned her face with her hand. "But I rather enjoyed it."

A dimple dotted her cheek when she smiled. However, every other aspect of her perfect visage had come undone with her efforts, like a once pretty doll with its seams unstitched and its fillings ripped out. Her hair no longer fell in neat waves. It tangled wild around her face, uncontrolled in a way she never would have approved or allowed but now seemed quite unconcerned with. Not a finger went to fix the errant strands or to straighten the collar of her dress.

Her face was flushed and splotchy, and at her temple, a vein pulsed. Broken capillaries had burst on the apples of her cheeks. Thin and red, they spread out beneath her skin like cracks in the earth.

A thin trail of blood trickled from her nostril.

She dabbed at her nose, and her fingers came away dripping and red. "I have not had to strain myself in this manner in such a long time." Her gaze shifted to Guy. "Not since the day you entered the underside of the graveyard without intending to return. I had to move ever so much dirt for the passageway to collapse."

Guy blanched. "You did that? You collapsed the tunnel on me?" His hoarse voice was no more than a whisper.

"How could you?" Irréelle cried. "How could you do such a thing?"

"Because he was going to run away. He would have exposed me!" Miss Vesper slipped a handkerchief from her pocket and wiped the blood from her fingers and face. She sniffed. "Besides, I can do whatever I like. He is no more than an extension of my imagination tied to old bones."

"He is real," Irréelle said with a rush of heat in her belly. The words came fast and fierce and unexpectedly. But that was how she thought of him, or at least wanted to think of him, even though it conflicted with how she thought of herself.

"He is not." Miss Vesper folded the handkerchief with still-shaking hands and tucked it out of sight, but Irréelle did not miss the embroidered initials.

Guy must have seen them as well, for he said, "We know your secret. We know what you are and will stuff you back in your coffin."

Miss Vesper's nostrils flared, but instead of looking angry, she looked terrified. Her hand lashed out like a claw, diamond ring glinting, and she snatched hold of Guy by the forearm. Her fingernails, so inappropriately pink, tore through his sleeve. "Never," she said, her face only inches from his. Fast breaths wheezed in her throat, as if the very thought of the casket's utter darkness and airless confinement was enough to suffocate her.

He pressed on. "We'll tell everyone you're a ghoul risen from the grave and drag you back to it."

"No more," she said, and whirled toward the hall, dragging Guy with her.

Irréelle staggered after, but took only a few steps. Without warning, Miss Vesper turned back. Her face was calm, her mouth curved into a dangerous smile. She let go of Guy and shoved Irréelle, knocking her into the wall, and then shoved her again, right into the closet beneath the staircase.

Irréelle crashed to her knees among the boots and boxes and the umbrella. She floundered on the floor, twisting toward the doorway.

Miss Vesper blocked the way. "Stay," she said.

The door slammed shut. The lock clicked into place. Irréelle found herself wrapped in darkness once again. Only a fine line of light edged under the door.

Guy shouted her name. She called back to him, but her voice bounced off the walls, a too-loud sound in a too-small space. From the hall, something clattered on the floor. Something else hit the door. Footsteps shuffled by and then receded.

"Guy," she said again, frantic. "Guy!" He made no response, and she could not help but think of the very worst. The thought was too awful, Guy too brave and whole, but all the same, Miss Vesper might do away with him.

With shaking hands, Irréelle brushed off her knees. Reaching up in the dark, she pushed at the coats hanging from the rod above and scrambled to her feet. Narrow and low-ceilinged, the space was tight even for someone as small as Irréelle. Her head smacked into the underside of the staircase. She yelped, bending her knees and hunching her shoulders to avoid hitting her head again.

Although she had heard them walk away, she pressed her ear to the door. On the other side, she heard nothing. No footsteps. No voices.

Miss Vesper could have been leading Guy back to the tunnels. She could have been calling the dirt to bury him again. And after, Miss Vesper would come for Irréelle. And Lass too. If not tonight, one day.

With both hands out, she fumbled in the dark for the doorknob. She twisted it this way and that. It would not open. If only she still had the skeleton key.

She threw herself at the door and banged her fists against it, hoping Lass would hear her. Again and again, she struck the wood. She and Guy had dug through a tree and into its hollow; it did not seem impossible that she could dig right through the door.

But no matter if she kicked or pounded or scratched, her assault left it undamaged. When she had worn herself out, her hands dropped to her sides. They throbbed.

She fell still. The quiet was smothering.

All was lost.

And then came a familiar scuttling sound. A burst of hope.

Something scratched against the wood. The door

shook in its frame and the doorknob rattled.

"Quick, quick," she said.

The lock snapped and the door cracked open. A sliver of light fell into the closet. Irréelle pushed back the door and slipped into the hall, peering each way to ensure Miss Vesper was not waiting there, ready to pounce. The Hand dropped from the doorknob to the ground.

"Aren't you clever? I feared you'd met your end." Irréelle looked down at the Hand. "Now, where has Miss Vesper taken Guy?"

The Hand darted down the hall and into the study. Irréelle hurried after, but when she entered the room, her face fell. It was empty. At first, she did not see the Hand, but she heard it scuffling on the other side of the desk. A scattering of papers shot into the air.

She crossed the room and rounded the desk. The top drawer gaped open. The Hand rifled through the contents, hurling out whatever it did not want.

"What are you doing? We can't waste time." Although the Hand seemed purposeful, Irréelle could only think of finding Guy, and he very clearly was not here. She turned to go, but the Hand reached out and caught the hem of her dress. It tugged her back. "Hurry, then," she said.

The Hand dug down to the bottom of the drawer and

emerged with a small book of poetry, which it heaved onto the desk. Where the binding creased, the book fell open. Pressed between the pages was a faded newspaper clipping, yellowed at the edges.

"What's this?" she asked.

The Hand stabbed its finger to the page. One corner was folded, and Irréelle smoothed it flat to reveal the entirety of a black-and-white photograph. She bent her head for a better look.

Miss Vesper gazed up at her from the newsprint, standing in a sapling's dappled shade that took up the whole of the picture. A wide smile lit up her face. A warm smile. Her hair was neither perfect nor untamed, but arranged in a simple style that fell somewhere in between. Beside her stood a man in a fine suit and tie. He did not look toward the camera; his eyes, his body, his hands all angled toward Miss Vesper. The tree's long, leafy branches framed their forms, entwined as neatly as the engraving inside Miss Vesper's ring and on her tombstone.

Below the photograph there was a single line.

Miss Arden Mae Vesper and Dr. Nicholas Montgomery Hauser announce their engagement.

"You spy on everyone, it seems," Irréelle said. "Miss Vesper should not have put you in her drawer if she did not want you going through her things." Or, she realized for the very first time, maybe the Hand had never been spying for Miss Vesper. Maybe it had always been trying to help Irréelle. After all, it led her and Guy to Miss Vesper's casket and later to her grave.

The Hand poked the old clipping again, tap, tap, tapping at the image of the scrawny tree, as if to make its point. She pushed the Hand aside gently, mindful of how fragile the paper was, soft at the edges as if Miss Vesper had handled it many times.

"Yes, I see." Or at least she was beginning to see, but she could not smooth everything out in her mind as she had smoothed the piece of paper. She was missing something, like looking backward in time at a faded memory, recognizing the shape of things but missing the details. She would have to think on it later. "We need to find Guy."

"I know where he is," said a familiar voice.

Irréelle's head snapped up. In the doorway stood Lass.

29

Fire

Irréelle jumped. "Oh, thank goodness."

"I'm sorry I didn't come sooner. I was tearing through Dr. Hauser's journals to see if I could find something to stop Miss Vesper. But then . . ." She paused, as if she did not want to voice her next thought, and then skipped over it entirely. "We need to hurry." Lass did not wait to see if Irréelle would follow and turned from the room, shoving a journal into the pocket of her coat.

Irréelle grabbed the Hand, which had crawled back into the drawer, and stuffed it into her pocket. She ran for the door and caught up to Lass in the hallway. "Where is he? What has Miss Vesper done with Guy?"

"They're outside."

Hearing this news, relief rushed through Irréelle's limbs, an unwinding of her muscles. There was nothing threatening outside. If Miss Vesper had taken Guy to the underside of the graveyard, they could have gone down any number of passageways, and Irréelle may not have found him until it was too late. Whatever Miss Vesper was doing in the backyard, it could not be as horrible as Irréelle had feared.

But then she caught the look on Lass's face and the grim set to her mouth.

They charged into the kitchen. Lass dashed to the back door, but instead of opening it, she pressed her back to it, arms out and barring the way. Her too-long sleeves drooped. "Don't panic, okay?"

Irréelle nodded. She was not the type to panic; at least, not the type to show it outwardly. Lass stepped to the side. Irréelle stared through the door's small window.

Outside, in the center of the patio, a massive fire roared in the stone pit. Flames licked the air, as if they were eager to be fed.

Irréelle could not see Guy, but the firelight threw shadows into the corners of the yard and he might have been anywhere in the darkness. Miss Vesper tossed wood into the fire's core and sparks rose into the sky. Leaking between the door and its frame came the scent of ash.

Irréelle pulled back from the window. Each time she blinked, the image of the fire blazed against her eyelids, and Miss Vesper's words ran through her head. "She threatened to burn my bones."

Lass's expression remained neutral, her voice numb and flat. "She threatened to cut off my limbs. That is, more of my limbs."

"More?" To Irréelle, it appeared they all were accounted for. A sense of foreboding wiggled its way down her spine.

"She promised to mend my limbs if I found the unmarked grave." Lass pushed up the sleeves of her coat. Her left hand was small and well shaped.

But her right hand was missing, the skin smooth where it poked out the end of the sleeve.

Irréelle's mouth dropped open, and Lass shoved her sleeves back down. She frowned. "It's a strange sight, I know. That is why I never showed you before."

"No, it's not that at all." Irréelle was the last person to think someone else strange. "But I'll have to explain later, as we need to stop Miss Vesper from throwing Guy to the flames." She glanced out the window again. The fire blazed higher.

"Follow me," Lass said, and tugged Irréelle away.

They could not go out the back door without Miss Vesper immediately seeing them, so they slipped out the front and sneaked around the side of the house, walking through the grass instead of along the path to mask the sound of their boots. They poked their heads around the corner.

Miss Vesper stood very still in front of the fire, so close she could tip into the flames. Guy sat on the patio by her feet.

"Why doesn't he just push her in?" Lass said.

Irréelle fell back to the side of the house, pulling Lass out of sight with her. "Quiet," she whispered.

"Well, he should." Lass folded her arms, the big sleeves flopping. "Before she does it to him."

"Guy would never do that," Irréelle said, even though it sounded exactly like something he might do, and then added, "I don't know if it would do any good anyway. N.M.H. awakened Miss Vesper from the dead. Can she die twice?"

Lass shrugged. "Worth a try, isn't it?"

Irréelle went hot all over, imagining her own bones aflame.

"I know, I know." Lass grew serious and leaned closer.

It felt quite nice, Lass's cool touch, how she whispered close to Irréelle's ear as if they were fast friends. "But what do we do?"

"We distract her. She still thinks I'm locked in the closet and she does not know you were with us in the attic."

"So she won't expect us," Lass said.

"Exactly." Irréelle lowered her voice. "And we have some other help as well."

"We do?"

Irréelle reached into her pocket. "I don't want to startle you, but I think I have something that belongs to you." The Hand crawled out of the pocket and up her arm.

This time Lass's mouth fell open. She looked at the Hand. Besides the scratch the owl had slashed across its knuckles, the Hand's color, shape, and size were an exact match to her left hand. "I can't believe it," she gasped. She plucked the Hand from Irréelle's arm and hugged it tight. "How do you suppose I'm to reattach it?"

"Not without considerable bone dust." At least that was what Irréelle imagined, if it was even possible at all. Perhaps they could find something in the journal Lass had taken from the attic. "But that will have to wait."

"Yes, of course it will." The Hand squirmed, feisty as always. "What is your idea?"

Once Irréelle laid out the plan, she and Lass pressed into the shadows, remaining on the side of the house. Lass squeezed the Hand to her chest again and then released it. As soon as it touched the ground, it scampered away, circling back to the front porch.

"Be careful," Lass said, staring after it, as if she could not bear to part with it so soon after being reunited.

Irréelle patted Lass's shoulder. "It will be okay." If the Hand listened to Irréelle's instructions, it would soon be opening the back door and leading Miss Vesper on a chase through the house.

They waited for the creaking of the door, for Miss Vesper to investigate, for an opportunity to grab Guy and run off into the night, anywhere else, whether they belonged or not. The Hand, Irréelle was quite sure, would have no problem finding them afterward.

And with Dr. Hauser's journal secure in the pocket of Lass's coat, they still had a chance of understanding his magic.

Irréelle tingled with impatience. She peeked around the corner again. Miss Vesper still faced away, poking at the fire with a stick.

At the same time, Miss Vesper snapped her head toward the house. The back door swung open. "Don't move," she said to Guy, and then took one step after another across the patio. She slipped out of sight into the house.

"Now," Irréelle whispered to Lass.

They crept through the grass to Guy. As they drew closer, Irréelle realized his ankles and wrists were bound with twine, and she broke into a run.

"You've got to go. You've got to get out of here," he said, but Irréelle bent to untie him.

"Not without you," she said.

"We are all in this together." Lass crouched beside Irréelle and did what she could to undo the knots one-handed. Guy's eyes widened. "We won't leave anyone behind. Including the Hand, which I think you have already met. My other hand, that is."

"It's yours?" Guy raised his eyebrow. "We really aren't on the best terms, but I won't hold it against you."

Irréelle could not believe it, but Guy grinned. Sweat dripped down his face, fire roared at his back, Miss Vesper would return any moment, and still he teased. Maybe that was why he seemed so real to her, and Lass too. They saw darkness, just as Irréelle did, but they brought their own light into it. They gave her hope, and maybe she offered them the same, which was *almost* like being real.

Somehow, Lass managed to untie the knots on his

ankles while Irréelle was still fumbling with the twine on his wrists. "Do you need some help?"

"Yes, yes," Irréelle said.

Beside them, the fire crackled. They were standing much too close for her liking. It licked at their heels as if it wanted to drag them in, crisp them up, and burn their bones. She redoubled her efforts and tugged out the knots.

Moments later the twine around Guy's wrists fell to the ground. Irréelle grabbed one arm, Lass took the other, and they pulled him upright. They wasted no time and tore across the patio, circling toward the side yard.

Irréelle's chest expanded with hope at the sight of the fence. Beyond it, the landscape stretched in all directions. In a world so large, there had to be someplace where the three of them would belong.

A firefly sparked past, fast and bright. A warm light leading them away from the house. Another one flew over their heads.

Their eyes (one pair very dark, one pair gray, and one pair muddled), lifted at the same time, drawn by the light. Fireflies dotted the sky like fiery stars.

And then they fell in a single rapid motion.

"Ouch," Guy said. He slapped at his arm. A tiny singed hole dotted the sleeve of his shirt.

"That stings," Lass said, swatting at her bare leg.

The fireflies gathered before them. They flashed orange. They flickered.

Guy and Lass stopped dead. Irréelle kept going. She was so close, so close. The gate was right there, just past the fireflies.

She stared at their small bodies. Only then did she realize they were not insects at all, but tiny flying embers of fire.

And they surrounded her, blocking the way to the front yard.

30

Into the Grave

Fire sparked around her.

Irréelle could neither advance nor retreat. The glowing embers burned too hot, they pressed too close. The air hissed.

She lashed out, for all the good it did. The specks of fire danced out of reach, slipping between her fingers and around her ankles, stinging her wherever they touched. It would be a slow end, to be burned up bit by bit. Of all the ways to go, she might have feared this most of all.

Sparks alighted on her dress and her arms. They scorched pinprick holes in the fabric and singed the hair from her skin. Irréelle shrieked and shouted, patting down her skirt.

A dark figure leapt through the sparks. Something swept protectively around her shoulders.

"Come on," Guy said, huddled under the coat beside her.

Heads down, they burst past the embers burning in the air. The sparks snapped and sputtered, chasing them away from the gate. Lass hollered at them to hurry, and they followed her around the side of the house, into the backyard once again.

They stopped short. Guy dropped Lass's coat. Irréelle's knees knocked unevenly.

Miss Vesper stood in the center of the patio, her face rage-red. She snapped her fingers, and the sparks of fire flared. They swirled once, like a galaxy burning, and then smashed into the fire pit.

Miss Vesper leveled her eyes at each of them in turn, first Irréelle, then Guy, and last Lass. They edged backward, but it only brought them closer to the fire pit, their heels nudging against the stones. The skin on the back of Irréelle's legs warmed unpleasantly.

Miss Vesper's gaze lingered on Lass. "So you've already determined to disappoint me. After only a few days' breath. And your Hand behaves no better."

Irréelle looked toward the house, hoping to catch sight

of the Hand. She did not see it sneaking across the patio or scampering in the grass. She did not hear its fingertips scuttling.

"I see how you are," Lass said. Her fingers went to the smooth skin on her arm.

It had taken Irréelle months and months to see so clearly. But now her eyes were truly open.

"And to think, I would have spared you. At least for a time," Miss Vesper said.

"Spare her still," Irréelle pleaded. "I will do anything you wish." Such was the love she held for her friends, a love that burned brighter than any bonfire Miss Vesper could build.

Three swift strides and Miss Vesper stood directly before her, pushing Guy and Lass out of her way. The tips of her shoes touched the toes of Irréelle's boots. Up close, the tiny veins on each of her cheeks appeared darker, irregular lines like cracked glass. Dried blood ringed her nostril.

Irréelle leaned away, listing toward the fire. One shove from Miss Vesper and she would land in the blaze. *Cut the tether. Burn your bones. Be no more.* The words came back to her like a struck match suddenly aflame.

"I will spare none of you."

Behind Irréelle, the logs shifted in the fire pit.

Blackened pieces of wood broke in two, and the structure collapsed. The fire hissed and smoked, stinging her eyes.

"Please. Please not the fire." Already, it felt like she was roasting.

"You have proven much too noisy," Miss Vesper said. The fire reflected in her eyes. She stepped back. "I would not want to disturb the neighbors with your screaming."

Irréelle flinched.

Guy thrust out his chin and straightened to his full height. He was almost as tall as Miss Vesper. "You can't say such horrible things to us. You can't speak that way."

With a flick of her wrist, Miss Vesper called to the dirt. It swirled up in a cloud, gathered from the cracks between the stones in the patio. It arced in the air and funneled toward Guy. He edged back, leading it away from Lass. It circled around him.

He swatted at the dirt, but it pressed closer, worming past his arms. He slapped his hands over his lips, but the dirt slipped between his fingers and filled his mouth completely.

"No, it is you who cannot speak." Miss Vesper brushed her palms together, though she had not touched the dirt.

Eyes wide, Guy coughed and gagged.

Miss Vesper was not through. She threw out her hands, and the ground shuddered. Beneath their feet, the individual patio stones shifted. Some sank into the earth. Others angled upward. The fire pit cracked, and embers and wood, still aflame, spilled onto the patio.

"Look out!" Lass cried.

Miss Vesper lifted her arms higher still. Everything trembled, the ground, the air, their bones.

Irréelle watched the yard transform.

The grass rippled, like some horrible monster was pushing up from beneath. The earth groaned, and then it split open.

A fountain of dirt erupted from the ground. The air smelled of soil and grass. Another explosion of dirt followed, and then one more. Until there were three deep holes in the ground, three mounds of dirt in the grass beside them. The holes were long and narrow, and rectangular in shape.

Miss Vesper had dug three graves.

She went for Guy first, wresting him away from Lass and dragging him toward an open grave. He barely struggled, hands to his throat, eyes flicking from Irréelle to the grave to Miss Vesper. Unable to speak, he grunted and moaned.

Irréelle flew at Miss Vesper. She had no time to consider the boldness of her actions.

Without even looking, Miss Vesper raised her palm. Dirt shifted, and Irréelle's foot sank into the ground as if she had stepped into quicksand. When she set down her other foot, the dirt parted in the same way and then sealed around her ankle. She tugged at her legs and wiggled her feet, but she could not move.

Guy looked back at her.

"I'm sorry," she said.

"No need to be sorry," Miss Vesper said. "You will be resting beside him soon enough."

And with that, she pushed Guy into the grave.

"No!" Irréelle cried. She knew nothing could be worse for him than to be buried again. She strained to lift her feet, but the ground held her firm.

Lass sprang forward. She was fast, and though the ground sucked at her feet under Miss Vesper's command, she avoided falling to the same fate as Irréelle. Her boots set down and then lifted again before they could sink. With her one hand raised, Lass ran toward Miss Vesper.

But Miss Vesper was taller and stronger and faster still. She stepped out of the way. Lass wobbled at the edge of the hole, the toes of her boots standing on nothing more than air. And then the dirt under her heels shifted. (It may have been Miss Vesper's doing, or the dirt may have crumbled all on its own, Irréelle could not tell.) Lass's feet slipped out from under her, and she tumbled headfirst into the grave.

Miss Vesper put her fingers to her neck, perhaps remembering the way it had snapped after tumbling down the staircase. One misstep, one push, and she would have fallen into the grave instead of Lass.

Irréelle bit her lip to keep from calling out. With Miss Vesper's attention elsewhere, she bent closer to her boots, the very tops of which protruded from the ground.

"I dug a separate grave for each of you, but it seems you would rather have the same one. I'm certainly not going to fish one of you out of there just to toss you into another." She kicked a clot of dirt down into the hole.

"Stop it! Stop it!" Lass's voice rose up from the grave, and Irréelle was glad to hear it, hoping it meant Lass was uninjured.

Irréelle yanked at the knots in her laces. They were tight and covered in dirt, but they were not as troublesome as the twine binding Guy's wrists and ankles had been. She untied the laces and pulled as hard as she could on her right leg. Her foot popped out of the boot. She did the same with her left.

In stocking feet, she tiptoed away from Miss Vesper. There was nothing she could do about her creaking bones.

Near the patio, she trod carefully to avoid stepping on a glowing ember. She leaned over the fire pit where the logs, in their disarray, still burned. Heat rushed across her skin. A few thick sticks burned on only one end, and she grabbed hold of one of these, lifting it out of the fire like a sword she had forged.

"Whatever will you do with that?" Miss Vesper said from behind her.

Irréelle spun around. She waved the burning stick in front of her. "Let them out or I will burn *you* to your bones."

Miss Vesper eyed the flame warily. "Put that down."

"I won't." She stabbed the stick forward. The flame flared, illuminating Miss Vesper's face and all the thin, twisting spider veins chasing each other across her cheeks.

Irréelle took a step forward, and another and another, slashing the flaming stick through the air and pushing Miss Vesper backward, toward the three graves. She brought her to the very edge of the first gaping hole.

Miss Vesper called a handful of dirt and sent it forward. It swirled around Irréelle's small torch, like black-winged moths to a flame. The dirt gathered closer, a dark swarm that smothered the fire.

Around the stick, her fingers went slack. It fell from her hand.

Miss Vesper loomed over her, a billow of skirts and

hair caught in the wind. The oak tree's branches shook. "Can you feel it in your bones? Your grave awaits you."

The words sank into her mind like heat set to a wrinkle, the jumble of her thoughts ironing out smooth. "Wait!" Irréelle cried.

Miss Vesper reached forward, hands latching on like cuffs. She forced Irréelle backward and held her over the open grave. It seemed a very long way down.

"Wait." Her feet slid on the dirt, and her bones tingled. Irréelle spoke in a rush.

"I know how to find the unmarked grave."

31

The Hawthorn

The night was creeping away, yesterday tumbling into today. Above them spread an in-between sky, the last glimmer of stars edged by the glow of the just-rising sun. A clash of deep purple and gold.

The bottom of the grave yawned up at Irréelle. She felt herself tipping, tipping, tipping, and at the very last moment, Miss Vesper yanked her onto steadier ground. She gulped in a breath. The air hung thick with dew and ash. It settled in her lungs.

She had barely regained her footing when Miss Vesper shook her by the arms. "Tell me. Tell me now. Where is the unmarked grave?"

"Let me go." Irréelle wriggled in her grip.

Miss Vesper uncurled her fingers from Irréelle's arms, but her eyes hooked into her just as sharply. "Go on, then. Tell me what you know, what you've been keeping from me."

"I've kept nothing from you." Irréelle backed out of reach, slowly, though she wanted to scramble away. "Can't you feel it?" If she paid careful attention, she detected sounds and vibrations in the night. Not the ones she could hear with her ears or touch with her hands, but the ones that buzzed in her bones.

The bone garden was not so very far away, and she had always assumed those were the bones she felt each time she stepped outside. She had not suspected that another set of bones rested much closer.

Ones that belonged to N.M.H.

"I feel *him*. Everywhere. No matter where I am. Yet still, he is lost to me." Miss Vesper's voice was laced with cracks and pits. "Don't play games or twist words. Lead me to the grave before I silence you forever."

Irréelle glanced over her shoulder. The oak tree stood tall behind her. She raced for it. Miss Vesper took her time, stalking after Irréelle like cornering prey.

Irréelle was so used to the skeletons in the underside of the graveyard, how gently they hummed and tugged at her heart. She was so used to listening. But now she reached out, feeling for the silent bones of N.M.H.

Just as Lass had explained when searching for the locksmith, Irréelle thought of all the things she knew of Dr. Hauser—someone who studied bones and crafted magic, someone who marked the world with hearts and loved nothing more than Miss Vesper.

Only it was very hard to concentrate with Miss Vesper going on and on.

"He's gone," she said, as if she still could not believe it. "He traded his life for mine, but I don't want it." Her voice rang hollow in the dawn. "I woke up beneath our tree as if I had only risen from a nap, not from death. I stretched my arms overhead. The sky had never looked so blue."

The words blurred. All Irréelle heard was *our tree*. Like the blackened oak in the graveyard, inscribed with their love. Like the branches entwined on the band of Miss Vesper's engagement ring. Like the sapling the Hand pointed to over and over again in the faded photograph. The tree must be here in the yard, only grown so much bigger now.

Irréelle reached the oak and circled it once, hands over the bark, eyes squinted and searching in the shadows where the sunlight, still thin and pale, did not touch.

Unwanted, Guy's words haunted her like the ghosts she did not believe in. *What if you find what she wants? What will she need you for then?*

She had only moments before Miss Vesper reached her, but she pushed away those thoughts and called to the bones. Irréelle could not worry about herself. Guy and Lass needed her.

Miss Vesper's voice curled through the overhanging branches. "And then I saw all the cracks in the world. Everything rushed back. Every detail. I remembered how careless I had been, hurrying down the spiral staircase when he called to me. I had wanted to see him so desperately."

The more Miss Vesper spoke of the past, the more Irréelle's bones whispered. N.M.H. must have been listening too. She warmed all over, drawn forward by his interest.

Miss Vesper stepped into her path. She touched her neck, long and graceful as if it had never been broken by the fall. "And it's what I want still. To see him. To be with him."

Irréelle huddled close to the tree, keeping it between them. "You searched the graveyard because you thought he'd be there."

"No. I created you little creatures to search the graveyard." Miss Vesper's voice rose in pitch.

"But he was never there." Flushed with the lightest tugging on her bones, Irréelle was certain of it, and not just because the watchman had told her so. Just like the headstones tilted toward each other in the cemetery, Irréelle had guessed N.M.H. would not want to be far from Miss Vesper.

But they had not been looking close enough. He would not watch over her empty grave; he would rest where she lived, right by her side.

Irréelle's bones would not lie to her.

Miss Vesper's head reared back. The light caught her eyes, and they flashed. "Of course he's there. Where else would he be?"

Irréelle had sensed him the very morning she picked tulips for Miss Vesper but had not even realized a set of bones rested so close. Irréelle's eyes tore over the yard and all the trees within it.

Her bones guided her straight to the little stepping stone path she had spied from the attic window. Grass grew long over the stones and many were cracked with age, but all at once Irréelle realized why they had reminded her of the underside of the graveyard.

Like the tunnel wending toward Miss Vesper's casket, hearts lined the way.

Irréelle faltered. If she went forward, she would be giving Miss Vesper everything she wanted and did not deserve. But that was not Irréelle's judgment to make, and it was not the reason for her hesitation.

In that moment, she paused so it could sink in, the fact that Miss Vesper would never magic her real, that Irréelle would never unravel the formulas in Dr. Hauser's journals.

I can be nothing more than I already am, she thought.

"I will bring you to the unmarked grave, but you mustn't harm Guy and Lass," Irréelle said solemnly. Freeing her friends, whom she loved even more than the idea of being made real, was what she wanted most.

"Yes, yes. Whatever you want," Miss Vesper said, edging closer.

"Promise." Irréelle would not let Miss Vesper trick her this time. "You must promise on Dr. Hauser's grave."

Miss Vesper flicked her hand, as if the fates of Guy and Lass were of little importance. "I promise on my most beloved." The words, even spiked with Miss Vesper's harsh tongue, rang true.

Turning, Irréelle followed the hearts beneath her feet and the one pounding in her chest. Miss Vesper stepped stone to stone after her.

At the end of the path, Irréelle stopped. There, a hawthorn grew willowy and slim, younger than the others in the yard. Its branches were full, the leaves summer-green and shiny. All the flowers were tiny and white, half-closed and waiting for the sunshine. An unruly lilac bush grew around it.

She shoved at the branches to get closer to the trunk. All the while, her bones hummed.

"Stay away from there," Miss Vesper said.

"Is this your tree?" Irréelle asked, but she knew it must be.

"We planted it before the wedding. Something to grow with us. What does that matter now?" Miss Vesper hissed as she approached.

At first Irréelle saw nothing, only a tree like any other, and she feared she had made a horrible mistake. Then she noticed a marking in the bark. It was distorted by growth and aged by the weather and all but hidden behind the lilacs. Irréelle pulled back the leaves to get a closer look.

A heart. And within it, someone had carved the initials *N.M.H.* ♥ *A.M.V.*

"He's here," Irréelle said.

32

A True Heart

Irréelle swelled with both excitement and dread.

Miss Vesper came toward the tree, so gently she seemed to float. Her eyes locked on the engraving. At first, she did not seem to recognize what it said, or else disbelief struck her mute.

"An unmarked grave that is very clearly marked," Irréelle whispered. "He marked the tree over your grave too, in just this way."

Miss Vesper pushed Irréelle out of the way, but half-heartedly. Everything about her wilted, limbs like petals that wanted to fall away. Her head tipped to the side. She reached out, as if the air was dense and it took all her strength to pass through it. Her hand touched the wood.

Miss Vesper gasped. The air snapped. Something stirred in Irréelle's bones.

"All this time," Miss Vesper said. "All this time my dear love was here. Here, resting beside me."

Irréelle swallowed, keeping quiet, backing away. One wrong word and she might still end up at the bottom of the grave, and if that happened, there would be no one left to help Guy and Lass. They would all be doomed, despite Miss Vesper's sacred promise.

Miss Vesper's gaze fell to the grass around the tree. Below the encroaching lilac bush, it was flat like the rest of the yard. Nothing to tell what lay beneath. No headstone, no marker. Only the inscription on the tree.

Ever so gently, Miss Vesper used her magic to part the grass and sift the dirt. It swirled in the air, graceful and fine, like dark snowflakes falling upside down, gravity reversed. The gold-and-purple dawn filtered through the leaves. In the odd light, Miss Vesper looked otherworldly, skin cast gray, the veins in her cheeks twisting like the finest roots. They grew longer, curling across her jaw.

She held her hands close to her heart. The tips of her fingers strummed the air. Another layer of dirt swept skyward, an orbit of little planets.

Irréelle took another step back, quiet as could be. Her

skin ran with static. Heat bubbled in her core, in her marrow and cinnamon blood. There was a thread, there was a tether, and, knowingly or not, Miss Vesper plucked it. Something in her chest pulled taut.

If she let herself, Irréelle thought she might be able to spin into the air like a mote of dust. Or fracture into a million particles. She clenched her teeth and held her stomach tight.

The dirt shifted faster, swirling, whirling, exposing bone. Against the dark earth, it gleamed.

Miss Vesper's hands stilled. Perhaps she had expected to find Nicholas Montgomery Hauser perfect and whole; perhaps she had not expected to find him at all.

She let out a breath and lifted the rest of the dirt away from the bones. The grave was shallow; the skeleton was dressed in a once-fine suit.

In all her time in the underside of the graveyard, Irréelle had seen many skeletons, but she had never seen one quite so sorrowful. Its eye sockets were more oval than round, its bottom jaw was unhinged from the top, and it smelled, not like rot, but like rain.

Miss Vesper trembled. "You should never have brought me to life unless you were still in it."

The skeleton said not a word.

"Nicholas," Miss Vesper said. "Wake."

The skeleton moved not an inch.

Miss Vesper's hands reached out like white spiders, knuckles bent, fingers twitching. "Breathe," she said. The air gasped, swirling around the hawthorn and shaking loose petals. "Breathe of the wind and with it soar fair skies."

Irréelle recognized the line from the poem Lass had found. *Could it be they were not a goodbye, but instead the very words used to give Miss Vesper life? Like a magical incantation? What of the second line, then?*

Slowly, slowly, the skeleton rose. Its skull lolled to the side.

But there was no spirit in those bones. Irréelle felt only its desire for slumber. It had no life, no flesh to return to, for all those years ago it had given everything it had to resurrect Miss Vesper.

A twisted laugh fell from Miss Vesper's too-wide mouth, the skin stretched so thin on her face her jaw shone through, bone-white and sharp. Her hair drained of color, glinting silver.

"Take of the life you have given me. Take it for your own," Miss Vesper said. Her body strained, as if she was doing all she could to pour her very soul into the upright skeleton. The bones rattled and shook.

Irréelle did not mean to, but she must have made some small sound, for Miss Vesper turned to her then.

"You are tethered to me. I will take from you what I have given." Her cheekbones protruded as if they might break free of her skin. "And when I have brought back my own dear love, you will be no more. You will return to dust and bone." She said the last words in a throaty growl. "All three of you."

"No!" Irréelle leapt forward. "You promised not to harm Guy and Lass."

"Oh, it won't hurt," Miss Vesper said. A smile sliced across her gaunt face. "Unless they struggle."

Threads of energy streaked through the air like lightning. They glowed midnight blue, flung out by Miss Vesper, and gold wound through them, a softer, gentler magic that must have come from the bones of Nicholas Hauser.

Irréelle slipped away from their reach, which poked and snapped with static. Miss Vesper grasped for the particles of bone dust and imagination she had gifted Irréelle. Something fluttered in Irréelle's chest, a fragile thing at the very center of her being that she felt more fully than she ever had before. She did not want to let it go.

Instead of backing up, Irréelle darted forward.

She thought of Guy and of Lass, and the light they carried

within them. She even thought of the Hand. It was tethered to Lass, but it was also a creature all its own, full of spirit. Irréelle could not see herself as clearly, whether something in her shone that bright or not. But she could feel, deep down, a vibration that was hers alone, unlike any other.

This will not be our end, she had promised Guy, and she meant to keep her promise.

Irréelle had no magic, but she had purpose. On mismatched legs, she ran straight through the coiling mass of Miss Vesper's power. It raked through her, intrusive and searching.

Miss Vesper lifted her arm as if to ward off Irréelle's attack, but Irréelle flew past her. She collided with the skeleton, which twitched and jerked under Miss Vesper's command, and Irréelle tumbled with it into the open grave.

"I'm sorry. I hope I have not damaged you." She untangled her limbs from the bones. "If you permit me, I will return you to your grave." Ever so gently, she straightened the skull, hoping it rested more comfortably.

"Don't touch him!" Miss Vesper dropped to her knees in the grass and shoved Irréelle out of the shallow grave. When her eyes fell on the skeleton, her face softened. She caressed the side of his skull as if she saw Dr. Hauser full of life.

Behind Miss Vesper's back, Irréelle scooped up a fistful of dirt. She sprinkled it in the grave and listened to the bones' quiet thrum. They were so very tired and wanted only to rest. A golden thread of light pulsed. Clods of dirt lifted from the ground, following Irréelle's lead, and began to fill the grave.

"What's happening?" Miss Vesper's head snapped up. She raised her hands, but perhaps she had grown too weak from all the magic she had called, for the earth continued to fall atop her and the skeleton.

"He's given his life for you," Irréelle said. "I don't think he will allow you to give it back."

"He must," Miss Vesper said, but the dirt only fell faster, clumping in her hair, covering her ankles. She swatted it from her eyes.

"He wanted you to have it." However, Irréelle did not think he would have liked how Miss Vesper chose to live it. Irréelle climbed to her feet, scrambling away.

"Don't leave me alone, Nicholas. Breathe," Miss Vesper said, the very word that brought the Hand to life. "Breathe of the wind—"

The skeleton lifted one bony hand.

What could the second line of the poem mean? Irréelle thought again. It flashed through her head. *Hush still the night and rest evermore thine eyes.* If it was not a goodbye (for he had written *thine eyes*, not *mine eyes*, she realized), and if the first line gave life—then the last line must take it.

"Hush," Irréelle said. Her breath shaky, the rest of the words caught in her throat.

She cared for Miss Vesper, even still. If these words cast Miss Vesper to her grave, if they allowed her to rest in peace at last, it would be for love, not revenge. The only way possible for the magic to work.

Recited by a true heart, love blooms welcome and love gentles farewell.

Irréelle's voice rang softly, like a bell. "Hush still the night and rest evermore thine eyes."

Miss Vesper's limbs trembled and quaked. She collapsed beside the skeleton and curled on her side. Her skin paled, cheekbones sharp in her narrow face, spider veins spreading over her neck and beneath the collar of her dress. Black lines slithered down the tops of her hands. She closed her eyes.

The dirt swelled and stormed. The air tingled with electricity. Irréelle's skin rippled. Her rib cage pinched tight, oxygen forced out of her lungs. Something snapped, loud and sharp like a thunderclap. It reverberated in her chest. The storm cloud of dirt fell upon Miss Vesper and her dear love, burying them close together.

Irréelle exhaled. She stared at the ground.

She had not even told Miss Vesper goodbye.

The sky brightened another shade, purple turning pink, gold edged with blue. Irréelle would very much miss the sunrise and all of the other whispers of magic in the world, Guy and Lass most of all, but she had done what she needed to save them. Or at least offer them a peaceful ending. Miss Vesper could no longer hurt them.

Irréelle's breath felt thin, her head light. She tilted her face to the horizon and waited for her bones to hush, evermore returned to dust.

33

Strange and Incredible

Sunlight kissed Irréelle good morning. It warmed her skin; it sank into her bones.

She did not turn to dust and blow away.

Her heart skipped fast and her legs wanted to do the same, reveling in the fact that she was alive. She hugged herself, every odd angle so familiar and shaped just right.

A clod of dirt hit her crooked spine.

Irréelle smiled. Earlier, something deep within her had fluttered. Now it thrummed. Something that had been there all along, only she had not been able to recognize it.

Another clump of dirt fell at her feet and broke apart. She swung toward the three open graves and limped toward the closest one. Dirt spit out of the grave and arced into the air. Still smiling, she leaned her head over the hole.

At the bottom stood Lass, knees bent, left arm up, a hunk of dirt in her fist. She was already launching the dirt when Irréelle popped her face over the side of the grave, so there was no time to stop her arm's progress. Irréelle jumped out of the way.

Lass bounced on her heels. "What's going on up there? Did I hit her? Did one of my dirt bombs save you?"

"Something like that," Irréelle said.

Guy stood there too, of course. He was coughing and spitting on the ground. The dirt fell damp and dark from his mouth. When Irréelle met his eyes he grinned wide, showing off teeth caked with mud. "Did I mess up my smile?"

"Not one bit," Irréelle said.

"What happened?" Guy asked. He scraped at his teeth with two fingers.

"There's time for that later. Help us out of here before anything else." Lass squinted into the sun as it poked higher in the sky.

"I'll be right back." Irréelle found an old ladder propped against the wall in the basement. It was missing one rung and another was almost in splinters, and she would not have used it in other circumstances, but it was the only ladder available and would have to do. She lugged it up the stairs and outside.

Lass climbed out of the grave with only one brief comment about the appalling condition of the ladder, and Guy, who followed right behind her, said nothing about it at all.

When they both reached the top, they scanned the yard for Miss Vesper. Their gazes fell on the mound of fresh-turned dirt beneath the hawthorn tree.

"Is that where the unmarked grave has always been?" Guy asked.

"Yes. And now it's Miss Vesper's grave as well." She would have to show them the newspaper clipping and explain the poem and tell them everything else Miss Vesper had said, but later.

"Is she gone, like really for sure gone? And buried nice and snug?" Lass asked.

Irréelle's throat burned. "Yes."

They nodded solemnly, all three of them watching the unmarked grave as if Miss Vesper might burst through the dirt. A leaf blew off one of the branches and landed on the mound.

Guy placed a hand on Irréelle's shoulder. "Let's go inside."

They turned away from the grave, walking past

Irréelle's boots still stuck in the ground and the crumbling fire pit where the fire had gone out. When they entered the house, they immediately heard something banging.

"What's that?" Guy asked.

"The Hand!" Irréelle said.

Lass was already running ahead, following the sound to its source. They found her in the dining room. In the china cabinet, the Hand knocked against the glass. As Lass approached, it stopped and pressed the pads of its fingers to the door. She unlatched the bolt.

"There you are." The Hand leapt for her shoulder. "Did Miss Vesper lock you in there?" Whatever gesture the Hand made, Lass seemed to understand. She nodded. "That's terrible."

Irréelle looked around the dining room, at the chandelier dripping with candles and the sturdy wooden table and the upholstered silver chairs that were as fancy as thrones. "We need to have a proper meal."

"A feast," Guy said.

"A celebration," Lass said. "But first . . ."

"A bath," Irréelle finished.

Each in turn, they bathed. (Guy went last and took the longest of all.) Skin scrubbed raw and clothing changed, they gathered in the kitchen.

"What's there to eat?" Guy asked.

Irréelle and Lass had already been through the cupboards and the pantry. "Potatoes," they said together. The basement was overflowing with them.

"What else?"

"Maybe there are enough ingredients to make bread." Irréelle heaved a bag of flour to the counter.

"And?"

"More potatoes," Lass said.

And then they proceeded to name all the different ways to cook a potato and got to work.

"Baked potatoes."

"Mashed potatoes."

"Potato potpie."

"Boiled potatoes."

"Potato soup."

"Potato cakes."

They talked as they baked and fried and boiled. Irréelle did not think any of them knew exactly what they were doing, but they did their best and managed not to burn anything except for the potato cakes. (And those, Irréelle thought, Guy burned on purpose. Although he bemoaned the blackened bits, he gobbled down every last one as he stood at the stove.)

Lass handed Irréelle a damp cloth and took one for herself. Together they wiped down the dining room table as Guy brought the bread from the oven.

Irréelle looked at Lass as she cleaned, considering her friend's face. "You look like you're our age."

"Maybe. She never said for sure. Only that she thought I looked to be a girl older than either of those pig-snouted girls next door."

"You mean pigtailed?" Irréelle asked. How long ago it seemed since she had spied the sisters through the fence.

"Miss Vesper most definitely said pig-snouted. And you know she always said what she meant."

Irréelle could not argue with that. The story made her smile.

They set the dining room table with the very best dishes, the bone china plates with the N.M.H. monogram, and the narrow glasses with the tall stems. They used the silverware with the curlicue pattern on the handle, and although the metal had lost its shine, Guy told them it was real silver and only needed a little polishing to look like new again.

In the cabinet, they found place mats and selected the white ones edged with lace. Although they were impractical, they matched the white hawthorn and complemented the sprig of lilac Irréelle had placed in a vase in the center of the table. (She had left daffodils on the unmarked grave as well.)

They carried platters and bowls from the kitchen to the dining room and filled each of their glasses with water. Guy and Lass sat at opposite ends of the long table and Irréelle took a seat in a chair between them. They piled their plates with bread and potatoes.

"Nothing has ever tasted better," Guy said around a mouthful of food.

"That's because all you had to eat was worms." But Irréelle could not deny how good everything tasted. A small smile danced on her face. "Maybe you would like worms for dinner."

Guy smacked his lips. "Oh, I much prefer them for breakfast."

"Gross! Let me enjoy my meal without hearing anything more about worms." Lass wrinkled her nose and took a sip of water.

"I could always scrounge them up for dessert." Guy snickered.

The Hand carried a roll to Lass and passed the butter to Irréelle. Guy called for another potato potpie. The Hand went back and forth over the length of the table, delivering what was asked for, and then settled by Lass's

301

elbow. It picked up her fork and scooped a mound of mashed potatoes from the plate.

"I don't think I want the Hand reattached after all." She opened her mouth and accepted the bite the Hand offered. "I'll never have to get up to fetch a glass of water again. Or carry a book from across the room or put out the light or . . ."

The Hand threw down the fork, and they all burst into laughter.

"Maybe," Irréelle said thoughtfully. "Maybe you should come up with a name for the Hand."

"Yes, yes!"

"How about Junior?" The Hand darted to the other end of the table, dipped its fingers into Guy's glass, and flicked water onto his face.

Irréelle smiled. "I would guess that means no."

"Absolutely not. It has to be a name pretty and sweet, or something French, like Irréelle." Lass clapped her hand to her opposite arm. "I know. Lassette."

Guy groaned. "I think it's more like *Sass*ette." The Hand directed another splash of water at his face.

"But Lassette is perfect. It means Little Lass."

"My name is French?" asked Irréelle. "How do you know?"

"My bones know French, so I know French. Your name means *unreal*. You know, because you're strange and incredible." Lass leaned her elbows on the table. "Come here, Lassette." The Hand did not budge, and Lass frowned.

Irréelle absorbed the meaning of her name. She waited for the fear to strike again, but instead understanding settled in her bones. The tether had already been cut. She did not exist in someone else's imagination and could not be extinguished with a single word. She had a heart and a brain and a will of her own. She would live just as any other girl might, with a fragile body that could be burned or buried, but not without a fight.

At the same time, she had always been right; she was unreal in a sense. And strange and incredible, and brave and stubborn too. Her life defied reason, built as it was from dust and bone and imagination.

It was a curious thing for her to accept, that no matter her origins, she was as fully real as any other creature in the world.

And so were her friends.

After they ate, they went into the study. Irréelle set to build a fire, and Guy and Lass helped stack the wood. The Hand, not to be left out, observed them from the mantel.

Once they kindled the fire and it began to blaze bright, they stepped back to admire it.

Irréelle sat down on one of the big chairs, the same way Miss Vesper had perched, straight-backed and cross-legged.

"That's not how you do it. Like this!" Guy flopped onto the other chair.

Lass leaned on the arm of Irréelle's chair and collapsed backward on it. Her legs dangled over the side. "I'm never getting up again."

Her head nudged Irréelle's leg, but there was plenty of room for them both. Irréelle scooted back and curled into the feather-stuffed cushions, just as she had always wanted to do. Only it was better, because she had her friends beside her. "I'm tired." She yawned and then closed her eyes without hesitation.

The scent of lilacs blew through the window. Their bones creaked as they settled more comfortably into the cushions.

And so, after they had a proper bath and a proper meal, together, they fell improperly asleep in the overstuffed chairs before the fireplace.

34

The Deepest Slumber

Yes, Guy snored.

But Irréelle snored louder, wrapped in the deepest slumber.

ACKNOWLEDGMENTS

I am still dizzy from spinning this story and appreciate everyone who held my hand and spun with me.

Suzie Townsend, I am grateful for you beyond measure. With your steadfast agenting magic, you navigated my sometimes-unsteady feet so that I never worried about falling. Thanks for being so wonderful.

Brian Geffen, while my storytelling may sometimes be subtle, I'll be more direct here. I am so, so thankful for you and your (very official!) editorial book sensing process— and more, for your kindness and support. Also, many thanks to Christian Trimmer, Rachel Murray, Katie (414) Klimowicz, Ilana Worrell, John Nora, and everyone at Holt who was tethered to this book in one way or another, and also Julia Lloyd, Cat Camacho, Lydia Gittins and Natasha Qureshi at Titan Books.

So many hugs for my dear friends, especially Kara (Melon!), and for my family—I love you all so much. Bill, you brought me notebooks that I filled with stories, and you melted my heart when I told you my book sold. Gram, you read me fairy tales over and over again, and you let me give you a villainous storybook name. Pop, you took me to the library and gifted me an antique desk and typewriter, as if you always knew I'd be a writer. Mom, you gave me your whole heart, you gave me the world—always and forever. You get my stories better than anyone, and it means everything to me. Cameron, you believed in me when I needed it most, and if not for you, this book would never exist. Nothing makes me happier than being with you (and I am keeping you evermore).

♥ C.N.S. + H.L.K. ♥

ABOUT THE AUTHOR

Heather Kassner loves thunderstorms, hummingbirds, and books. She lives with her husband in Arizona, waiting (and waiting and waiting) for the rain, photographing hummingbirds, and reading and writing strange little stories. *The Bone Garden* is her debut novel.

OTHER WORDS FOR SMOKE
Sarah Maria Griffin

From the author of *Spare and Found Parts,* described as "fierce and fearless" by V. E. Schwab and "beautifully written and compelling" by Marian Keyes, comes a story of a haunted house, magic behind the wallpaper, and the strangest summer ever.

The house at the end of the lane burned down, and Rita Frost and her teenage ward, Bevan, were never seen again. The townspeople never learned what happened. Only Mae and her brother Rossa know the truth; they spent two summers with Rita and Bevan, two of the strangest summers of their lives...

"Sarah's gorgeous prose will haunt you" Christina Henry

"A fascinating coming-of-age story" Charlie Jane Anders

"Griffin's hallucinatory novel creeps under the skin, unnerving readers while urging them forward" *Booklist* starred review

A DARKER SHADE OF MAGIC
V. E. Schwab

Most people only know one London; but what if there were several? Kell is one of the last Travelers—magicians with a rare ability to travel between parallel Londons. There's Grey London, dirty and crowded and without magic, home to the mad king George III. There's Red London, where life and magic are revered. Then, White London, ruled by whoever has murdered their way to the throne. But once upon a time, there was Black London...

"Marvellous" *Publishers Weekly* starred review

"Spellbinding" *Starburst*

"Smart, funny and sexy" *Independent*

WINTERSONG
S. Jae-Jones

The last night of the year. Now the days of winter begin and the Goblin King rides abroad, searching for his bride…

All her life, Liesl has heard tales of the beautiful, dangerous Goblin King. They've enraptured her mind, her spirit, and inspired her musical compositions. Now eighteen and helping to run her family's inn, Liesl can't help but feel that her musical dreams and childhood fantasies are slipping away.

But when her own sister is taken by the Goblin King, Liesl has no choice but to journey to the Underground to save her. Drawn to the strange, captivating world she finds—and the mysterious man who rules it—she soon faces an impossible decision. And with time and the old laws working against her, Liesl must discover who she truly is before her fate is sealed.

"Fantastic" *Publishers Weekly* starred review

For more fantastic fiction, author events,
exclusive excerpts, competitions, limited editions and more

VISIT OUR WEBSITE
titanbooks.com

LIKE US ON FACEBOOK
facebook.com/titanbooks

FOLLOW US ON TWITTER AND INSTAGRAM
@TitanBooks

EMAIL US
readerfeedback@titanemail.com